BIRMINGHAM
DISCARDED
BOOK
ST
PUBLIC
IBRA
IES

BILL OF INDICTMENT

Mark Harding, a young Harley Street psychiatrist, becomes engaged to the lovely young fashion journalist Veronica Lloyd. But just three months later, his world is shattered when Veronica is arrested for the murder of her landlord, businessman Sam Laing. Unknown to Harding, Veronica used to be Laing's mistress, and he forcibly resumed the relationship under the threat of telling Harding of her past.

Although Harding's old friend Detective Inspector Richard Morris wants to help, Veronica's fingerprints on the dagger and footprints at the scene of the crime seem to be damning evidence. Added to which, she admits to committing the murder!

By the same author

The Healing Knife
Surgeon's Symphony
They Came by Appointment
All This and Surgery Too
A Surgeon at Large
Surgery Hold the Door
A Surgeon in Rome
A Surgeon in California
A Surgeon in New Zealand
Appointments in Rome
Surgeon under Capricorn
Surgery and Crime
Tales of Ten Cities
A Surgeon in Australia
Punishment Deferred
Man Without Label
Alias Doctor Holtzmann
City of Cain
The Imperfect Surgeon
Of Guilt Possessed
Nothing Sacred
A Stranger in Harley Street
A Skeleton for my Mate
The Beloved Nemesis
Tell Your Grief Softly
On the Wings of Angels
The Sins of Andrea
Return from the Valley
Sheilagh of Buckleigh Manor
Every Sweet Hath its Sour
Of Men and Medicine
Pretty Polly
Mary, Mary, Quite Contrary
A Stranger in His Skull
No Man is Perfect
Crimson Eclipse
A Change of Heart
Innocence on Trial
The Price of Prejudice
The Killer Microbes
Double Identity
A Smile Through Tears

BILL OF INDICTMENT

GEORGE SAVA

ROBERT HALE · LONDON

First published in Great Britain 1986

ISBN 0 7090 2653 6

Robert Hale Limited
Clerkenwell House
Clerkenwell Green
London EC1R 0HT

Photoset in North Wales by
Derek Doyle & Associates, Mold, Clwyd.
Printed in Great Britain by
Dotesios Printers Ltd., Bradford-on-Avon, Wilts.
Bound by WBC Bookbinders Limited.

PROLOGUE

Veronica sensed more than heard her room door opening. She was not asleep and almost instinctively she turned towards the door. The huge frame of Samuel Laing cast a shadow in the dim light of the moon filtering through the French windows. She shrank in fear at what was going to happen. She knew well enough what was to follow when Samuel Laing forced his way into her room; knew only too well that she would somehow be compelled to partner him in one of his hideous sex-orgies.

By nature she was a quiet, gentle woman and could not recall ever having loathed a human being as she loathed this man.

Samuel Laing approached her bed and without a word pulled off the bed covers so that the naked body of Veronica shook with terror. "Come on, love, make room for old Sam!" The voice was calm but menacing all the same.

"Don't touch me, please!" Veronica sat up and spread her arms round her naked belly in an effort to cover herself somewhat. "Won't you ever get it into your head that I don't wish to have anything more to do with you? You have enough women to satisfy your varied tastes. Can't you, won't you leave me in peace?" There was genuine pleading in her voice.

"No, my dear, I've no intention of leaving you in peace.

You're still my favourite bird, you know. And somehow you manage to satisfy me better than any of the others. You should be damned proud of that."

"O' God, I'm not a whore, and you know it. Only your perverted sexual senses put me in the class of your other string of whores."

"If you aren't a whore what are you? A lady?" His sarcasm was scathing.

"Yes, I am a lady in the eyes of other people."

"You mean in the eyes of your head-shrinker fiancé – what's his name – Mike Harding? I wonder whether he'd think you're a lady if he knew all about our game – eh?" Laing gripped Veronica's bare shoulders with his strong hands.

"You mean to tell me that your head-shrinker fiancé has not yet made love to you?" He grinned. "Well, I am going to show you once again what a man feels like. You should teach him the way I have been imparting the art of love-making to you. You know, the Anglo-Saxon way of brute force."

"You are a beast, a maniac!" she hissed. She bit her lips because she knew that she should not have used that word, but it was too late. Laing heard it and a fierce light shot through his eyes. Abruptly he raised his hand which made a half-circle and shot violently across her face. It caught her square across the cheek and mouth bursting her lips. A small trickle of blood began oozing from her lips and her cheek became red-blue from the slap. Veronica collapsed onto the bed and began to cry of despair.

"Why don't you kill me," she whispered.

"I won't kill you, Veronica. You are the only woman who makes me feel so bloody virile and a little bit of brutal force is a part of the Anglo-Saxon way of love-making. You should know that by now."

Saying that Laing rolled his huge frame on top of her and thrust savagely into her inside. Veronica screamed again from the pain his brutal love-making was causing her. His animal-handling of her all but choked the breath out of her. Exhausted and half-spent, she passed out in complete oblivion.

When she awoke the next morning Laing was gone and she felt a dull headache which gradually seemed to reach bursting point. Nauseated and incredibly tired, she went to the bathroom and took some tablets. Soon after, her headache eased a little. She dressed casually and went out.

For how long she walked she did not know, but she realised that she was standing in front of the curio shop in King's Road, Chelsea. She walked in and looked at the display of various objects spread out on the table. She fixed her gaze on a bejewelled Arab dagger which sparkled in the light of the morning sun, and taking it in her right hand, asked the shop keeper how much it cost.

"Oh no Miss, this is not for a lady like yourself. It's razor-sharp and dangerous, and would probably kill a man by itself!" he laughed at his joke.

"How much?" she repeated, raising her voice.

"Seven quid." The man named an exorbitant price, hoping it would be above her means.

Veronica withdrew a ten pound note from her purse, and still clutching the dagger, gave it to the man. "Keep the change," she said and walked out of the shop.

She felt she could not walk back to her flat. Exhaustion had completely overcome her. She hailed a passing taxi. Inside the cab she sat back and relaxed for the first time in hours. Her body ached physically. There must be the usual bruises all over her. At moments she still had the sensation of Laing's grasping fingers digging into her flesh. But it was the feeling of complete degradation, of having been so terribly sullied, of which she could not rid herself. She would have a long bath the moment she returned. Hot and long.

ONE

Thursday, September 7th – a day I shall remember all of my life for more reasons than one. It started in the usual way with a sunny morning promising to blossom into one of those rare autumn days which justifies the Englishman's greeting of strangers with 'nice day!'. I thought it was going to be a nice day for me too, but how wrong was that assumption I found out almost the moment I stepped out of my house.

In the morning, a simple case of juvenile delinquency in which I was summoned to give evidence as an expert psychiatrist, turned out to be a long, unpleasant Court proceeding. The rape of a minor by her foster-father – with me in the witness-box for over two hours of cross-examination – trying to prove that the defendant was not insane and knowing full well the gravity of the crime he was committing. In the afternoon, after an unsuccessful attempt at finishing a dull lunch, my car's steering-wheel broke down and I narrowly avoided a head-on collision but smashed the car into a side wall. Dealing with the accident took three hours and I was late for my patients' appointments in my Harley Street rooms. Three of the patients had left furious – so my secretary informed me – but those that waited still kept me until eight o'clock in the evening. I had to cancel a dinner-date with a colleague and almost collapsing with exhaustion, I managed to drag myself home and gulped down the dinner, good as usual, that old Maggie, my housekeeper, had ready waiting for me.

And that night the phone beside my bed startled me from my sleepless reveries with its shrill ringing. I let it ring for a few seconds unable to move and still staring at the invisible ceiling, when a polite coughing from Maggie's room told me that the phone's ringing had wakened her too, poor soul. I lifted the receiver and switched on the bedside lamp at the same time.

The voice at the other end of the line sounded very official and impersonal; "Doctor Harding?"

"Speaking."

"Doctor Mark Govan Harding?" the impersonal voice repeated.

"Yes," I shouted, this time not trying to disguise my annoyance at being disturbed at such an ungodly hour. "Who else?"

As a doctor, I suppose a call at any hour of the night should not have provoked such violent reaction in me. But my G.P.'s days lie some way behind, and my present practice – I am a consulting psychiatrist and medical psychologist – is not the type that leads to urgent midnight summonses. Of course, old Jan Maggogh might have become savage, or one of the other patients might have been misbehaving ... But it was unlikely, and in any event I never took kindly to being called out of bed. Certainly the message was the last thing in the world I could have expected.

"Sorry, doctor, for calling you at such a late hour, but ..."

"That's all right," I interrupted the late intruder, trying in the meantime to calm myself. "What can I do for you?"

"This is Sergeant Collins of the C.I.D. Central Office. I am calling on behalf of Miss Lloyd, whom I think you know."

"Who did you say? Veronica Lloyd? My fiancé?" I sat up in my bed covered with cold sweat. A sudden fear gripped my whole being. "What's the matter with her?" I managed to blurt out, visualising for a moment my Veronica's body bleeding to death, lying unconscious somewhere in the country following a car accident. "Is she hurt?"

"No, doctor, she is not hurt," the police sergeant answered evenly. "Miss Lloyd has been arrested!"

"Arrested?" My temper began to rise again. If this was someone's idea of a joke it was in very poor taste. "Sergeant," I took up the conversation, "it must be a mistake. It has to be."

"No, sir. It is not a mistake. Miss Lloyd was arrested an hour ago and she asked for you to be informed. That's why I'm telephoning you."

"But, arrested – Why? On what charge?"

"I'm not at liberty to tell you any more. You'd better get in touch with the Inspector in charge of the case."

"And who is that?" I asked, still certain it was a grisly joke.

"Detective Inspector Richard Morris of the C.I.D. Central Office."

"Oh, Morris!" My voice must have sounded relieved. What a godsend it was that Inspector Morris happened to be a friend of mine. "Thank God!" I said more for my own benefit.

"Can you put me on to Inspector Morris?"

"One moment, doctor."

Detective Inspector Richard Morris of the C.I.D. Central Office – though he won't thank me for setting down also, his second name, 'Cuthbert', for all the world to see – happened to be a good friend of mine, but I won't go into that now; I shall have a lot to say about him later. However, the fact that he was in charge of Veronica's case was a great comfort to me. At least I would know about the circumstances of my fiancé's arrest and whose mistake it was. That it was a mistake I had no doubt whatever.

"Mark?" Inspector Morris's friendly voice came through the receiver. "I'm terribly sorry that it's got to be me who has to give you such bad news about Veronica."

"I'm glad it is you, Dick. But tell me – it is a mistake, isn't it – I mean Veronica's arrest?"

"I'm afraid not, Mark." His voice sounded almost apologetic. "Far from it."

"But – but on what charges? Motoring offence?" I suddenly recalled Veronica's love for speeding. "Has she run over somebody?"

"No, Mark, not run over somebody." There was a silence as if Inspector Morris were finding it difficult to continue with the conversation.

"For God's sake, man, can't you be more explicit?"

"Yes, Mark. I'm trying."

"Well?"

"Veronica has committed murder!"

Strange how people react differently to a sudden, unexpected shock. For a moment I remained stunned, biting my lips until I drew blood trying hard to suppress a cry.

"Mark? Are you there? Are you all right?"

"Yes," I answered flatly. "Is Veronica all right?"

"Yes, she was a moment ago." I detected a curious note in Dick's voice. "Don't you wish to know the name of the man she supposedly killed?"

"No, I don't believe any of it." It was an answer more to my own thoughts than to Dick's question. "Veronica couldn't hurt a fly, let alone kill a man ..."

"Mark, you'd better come down here as soon as you can," the Inspector was saying, but it was quite a few moments before I could answer.

"Yes, Dick," I said evenly, "I'd better come." Yet the shock was so great that I simply could not move from my bed but sat there staring at the receiver I still held in my hand.

Old Maggie, who had come into my room quietly, was staring down at me, her once blue eyes full of grief and sympathy for me.

"You heard all, Maggie?"

My housekeeper nodded. "I heard it, Doctor Mark." Her voice was warm and understanding.

"Veronica a murderess? NO!" I shouted. "Not Veronica." I slammed the receiver that was still in my hand.

"I don't believe it either, Doctor Mark," said Maggie soothingly and went out of the room.

I was still sitting on my bed in a kind of stupor when Maggie came back with a cup of tea in her hand.

"There you are, Master Mark, drink that. It'll do you the world of good – a nice hot cup of tea."

Good old Maggie! She was more like a mother to me than a housekeeper. "Thank you, Maggie," I said, taking the cup and starting to drink the hot liquid that began to warm my frozen guts and helped me return to reality.

Veronica has been my fiancé for exactly three months and five days. She's a lovely girl in every way. I was staying for the week-end at a friend's country house. It was Saturday evening and I was sitting on the veranda in the semi-darkness with a glass of whisky and soda in my hand, thinking of nothing, just staring into the infinite darkness and relaxing.

"My friends tell me you're a doctor – a psychiatrist?" A shadow obscured my view.

I stood on my feet. "Sorry, I didn't hear you coming," I said, blinking once or twice and staring quite unashamedly at the lovely apparition. The girl was tall, dressed in pink and white, with her light blonde hair falling generously over her bare shoulders. When she spoke again her voice sounded determined and warm.

"My friends tell me you are a good psychiatrist."

"They are my friends too, and ..." I laughed, "like all good friends they are exaggerating." I laughed again. She was definitely as good to look at as her voice sounded. Blue eyes, full sensuous mouth, velvety white skin and shoulders to match her remarkably shapely breasts.

"Quite a girl," I told myself silently.

A faint smile opened her lips slightly. "What is the verdict of ... your examination?" she asked mockingly. "Am I okay?"

"Sorry. I didn't mean to be rude," I said, blushing slightly.

"Why sorry? Don't you find me attractive?"

"Most attractive," I laughed again, regaining my composure. She certainly had a nice sense of humour to boot. A wonderful combination.

"Forgive my boorishness, but let's begin at the beginning. My name is Mark Harding." I held out my hand. Her hand was warm and strong, not the usual soft feminine texture. I liked it very much.

"I am Veronica Lloyd."

"Pleased to meet you." We both laughed. "Can I get you a drink?"

"Yes, thank you. Dry Martini, please."

And that was how we had met and we got along well together right from that Saturday evening at our mutual friend's country house. We went out and about frequently and then later we became engaged. I find it difficult to write about her thus and describe her, because I feel that any word picture I try to give of her will suffer from two major defects. The first is that anything I say is likely to be taken as biased; the other is that no words of mine could do justice to her. I will try and let her many virtues appear of themselves as I tell this tale. At any rate, I have described roughly what she looks like – at least in my eyes. What she means to me is even harder to put into words. Psychiatrists do not perhaps fall in love easily, but when they do, it hits them very, very hard.

Once I had got the damaged Jaguar, which was still running, out of the garage, I made short work of the journey. I doubt if even I, who have a reputation for loving speed for its own sake – as, I regret to say, the endorsements on my old driving licence in the thirty-mile-an-hour limit's days show – have ever moved so fast before. The roads were clear, and though one or two patrol policemen flashed their lanterns at me and brought thoughts of police cars to my mind, I arrived very quickly at Scotland Yard.

Inspector Morris must have given some very emphatic instructions, for it was the first time in all my many visits there that I did not have to fill in a visitor's form. As soon as I uttered my name, the duty policeman called a messenger and I was taken up to Dick's office. To my disappointment, he wasn't there.

It was a neat little room and I wondered whose it was. Inspectors of the C.I.D. do not have offices of their own, in spite of all that is said by crime writers. Scotland Yard is far too crowded for such a luxury. My mind was churning round and round with anxiety and I just had to do something to occupy my attention. Yes, I have to confess I took to snooping. I looked in the 'in' and 'out' baskets on the desk and found that the memos were addressed to Superintendent Coolhurst. So that was it; while the respected superintendent slept the sleep of the just and hard-working, his subordinates filched his office. It is an index to the state of my mind at that moment that I thought this a good joke and chuckled, though the sound of my own laughter startled and annoyed me.

Inspector Morris came in not more than five minutes later, though it had seemed an age. He was looking drawn and worried, as though he had something very unpleasant on his mind, and he gripped my hand firmly and warmly but in complete silence. So he stood for an appreciable interval, saying nothing and apparently at a loss how to begin. By now I couldn't stand it any longer.

"For God's sake, Dick, say it's all been a ghastly mistake!"

"I wish I could, Mark. God knows how I wish that it *was* a mistake."

"Veronica a murderess?" I stared at my friend. "Dick, you know Veronica yourself. Can you imagine her committing murder?"

"Yes, I know. It is hard to imagine, but I have no choice. You see ..." he licked his thin lips; I had never seen him so utterly miserable and dejected. "... you see, we had to arrest her on a murder charge because of the overwhelming evidence."

If he had used that famous right hook which once won him the amateur middleweight championship, he could not have dumbfounded me more. I stared at him utterly dazed, unable to think, let alone speak. He stepped forward and pushed me gently into a chair.

"Steady, old man. I can imagine how you're feeling. I wish to God it was someone else's case," he said in a soft voice.

I pulled myself together with an effort. "No, Dick," I said. "Thank God it's you dealing with the case. But in Heaven's name, on what evidence?"

He turned his head away from me and with his face still

averted he spoke to me in what made every effort to sound like a professional voice.

"You know that before we charge anyone with murder we must have a pretty fair amount of evidence."

"And you have it against Veronica?" I spoke as if in a dream.

"Unfortunately, Mark, we have. Quite overwhelming."

I felt cold and then immediately grew feverishly hot. Murder! Veronica on a murder charge! That was the only thought in my mind. I could not think of anything else. Until now I still had some hope that all this nightmare had been a grisly mistake. The room became blurred and misty before my eyes. I forgot all about Dick. I could only see Veronica as I had last seen her – when would that be? Barely forty-eight hours before – smiling and waving as she had sent a final goodbye to me from the porch of the house where she had a first-floor flat.

Then the reaction came. It was absurd, completely and utterly incredible. It was some fantastic mistake, or the whole thing simply was a nightmare and I would awake at any moment. It had to be! The same conviction of Veronica's innocence that had gripped me at my home when I first heard about the case came over me now. My vision cleared. I saw Dick with his head cast down, apparently afraid. Yes, it was a godsend that he was on this case. If anyone could help her, he would.

"I'm sorry, Dick," I said in a spent voice. "I know how you must be feeling."

"Yes," he answered, after a pause. "It was my job – the worst I've ever had to do. But it could not be avoided."

"I suppose not. You'll try to help her though. Won't you?"

"I'll do my damnedest. I like Veronica, you know that."

"Yes, I know, Dick." I gripped his hand and held it. "But help me, please. Help me to understand this whole, bloody mess!" I had nearly cried "help me to wake up quickly!" but stopped myself just in time.

My friend nodded slowly and leant forward wearily on his desk.

TWO

I am not going to tell Inspector Morris's story in his own words as he related it that night. It has always been a miracle to me how some people seem able to recall, weeks later, every word of a conversation of which they have made not a single note. I personally cannot remember anything of Dick's actual phraseology. True, here and there a phrase has become etched in my mind, but the total is very small. So, it is better to set down a reconstruction of the events as Inspector Morris described them to me. Perhaps he did not tell me everything on that one occasion, but that does not matter. All I am proposing to do is to write out an account on all the data I have.

Before I do that, though, it will be better if I introduce Inspector Richard Morris and myself in more detail. I am not a trained journalist or writer and I am amazed how very hard it is to give a picture in words even of someone very close to you. The things one sees in a friend are not those that the impartial observer sees, but I shall just do my best.

Let me deal with Richard Morris first, because for this story he is by far the more important person. I first met him some years ago when I was deputizing for the divisional surgeon in one of the south London suburbs. Dick was a detective-sergeant then, dealing with all the petty crimes and minor offences that make up the routine of police work. He did his work very efficiently and it was no surprise to anyone when he was transferred to Central and, shortly afterwards, promoted to detective inspector.

In appearance Richard Morris is one of those spare, broad-shouldered men who look short for their height. Yet he is all of six feet one inch in his stockinged feet. His face is rather colourless, with prominent cheekbones and a determined jaw, and his mouth is thin-lipped, though there is no suggestion of cruelty about it. His eyes are of a rather indeterminate blue but rather attractive. He is, actually, one of those men whose personality strikes you long before you become aware of actual physical features. I know of no one who gives more immediately the impression of confidence and rock-like reliability. You feel at once that when he says a thing he means it and won't go back on it, and that if you were in trouble here is the man you would like to be able to confide in and lean upon.

When you begin to know Inspector Morris better, you realise that his rather emotionless face conceals an exceptionally keen mind that is perfectly honest with itself. He is not one of those policemen who are out for convictions at all costs. When he acts it is because he has convinced himself first, but even then he is ready to listen to arguments and alter his mind if necessary. If he gives you his trust and confidence he does so absolutely. In one word, Dick is a thoroughly *likeable* human being.

When I try to introduce myself, I hardly know what to say. I cannot possibly give even an objective account of myself. To put it simply, I am an ordinary Englishman in appearance, with the name of Mark Govan Harding. I qualified as a medical practitioner and received my M.R.C.S. and L.R.C.P. from the Royal College of Surgeons in what seems to me an astonishing number of years ago, and then held house physicianships and did odd jobs as an assistant or locum to sundry general practitioners up and down the country, before sitting for my M.D. London. Not long afterwards I got my first consulting appointment as a psychiatrist with one of the Regional Group of Hospitals. I have known most of the ups and downs of the medical profession under the National Health Service, but they don't belong to this story.

Meeting Richard Morris stimulated my interest in medical jurisprudence and criminology. We were concerned on a murder case and the mere facts of being actually on an investigation roused all my enthusiasm. Dick's quiet abilities, too, impressed me. But the life of a divisional surgeon or a coroner did not appeal to me and so I have remained no more than an amateur in the field.

That is all I need to say about myself. Many other things will probably, quite accidentally, emerge later.

From what I have said about Inspector Morris, it should be clear the shock I felt. He had arrested my fiancée – and I knew him to be a man of the highest integrity and mental and moral honesty. If I had just been told that Veronica had been arrested by the police, I should have felt profoundly shocked, but I should also most probably have been filled with rage at another egregious official blunder. As it was, to condemn the arrest offhand as a blunder, appeared quite impossible.

There it was. The whole affair looked as black as it could be – a position from which there was no possible thought of escape. Yet curiously I also derived a little comfort from the fact that Dick was in charge of it. Never for one moment did I believe in Veronica's guilt. It was just a terrible mistake. And just because Dick had the case in hand there would be no difficulty in getting that mistake recognized for what it was, as soon as it could be demonstrated. Inspector Morris would not try to hinder a thorough investigation. I even felt, as he proceeded with his story, that he might be glad if a flaw *could* be found. He hated the whole thing – of that I was quite sure. For he certainly was a dedicated policeman – but he was equally a dedicated friend.

Having got the preliminaries over I must get back to the main track of the story. As I say, Inspector Morris did not tell me all the facts at that time, for the very adequate reason that he did not know them then. What follows is just a straight account of the case that was built up against Veronica.

My fiancée lived on the first floor of a row of converted Regency houses, in one of the quieter streets of Bloomsbury. She never gave anyone any cause for complaint. It was true that sometimes she came in very late, but then journalists keep curious hours and the night is often more important to them than the day. She was a freelance with connections with some of the fashion magazines, for she sketched very well and could illustrate her articles. Not only did she cover the fashion shows; she also attended first nights and social gatherings in order to give lively accounts and sketches of what was being worn by the great, the rich and the jet sets. Like so many of these converted houses, the one in which Veronica lived had a communal staircase and there were no separate front doors to the individual flats. Her downstairs and overhead neighbours, therefore, knew perhaps more of her than is usual among flat dwellers and they agreed that she was a quiet young woman who gave no rowdy parties and, indeed, rarely had visitors at all.

So much, then, for the principal character and her immediate background. A detective novelist, looking for the 'least likely person' on whom to pin a crime could hardly have found a more suitable victim.

Veronica's quietness as a tenant was not equalled by the neighbour on her right, also on the first floor. Samuel Laing was a noisy man who threw parties that had long plagued his other neighbours, but as it appeared that he owned the house in which he occupied a flat, as well as two on either side of it, little enough could be done. Rowdy parties were not the only feature of Laing's life. When he was not entertaining en masse, he apparently had visitors at all hours of the day and night – and particularly at night. Cars called at Laing's house as late – or as early – as three or four o'clock in the morning. Many of them were loud sportscars, which did nothing to add to Laing's popularity among his neighbours.

On the night of Thursday, 7th September, Samuel Laing had a number of callers between eight and half past ten in the evening, and then there was a lull before the next batch started about midnight. During the lull he retired to seek a little rest. This, his man said, was his invariable habit. He did not undress fully and go to bed, but slipped on a dressing-gown and lay down on a divan. Hobart, his man, insisted that Laing would see no one between halfpast ten and quarter to twelve; it was a rule that had never been broken.

At ten minutes to midnight, the first of the second group of visitors arrived – a man named Purlin, who was a restaurant manager. Laing had not emerged from his retirement, but his manservant, seeing that the prescribed time was past, went to the room to call him. It was then that the discovery was made.

George Purlin had been left in the lounge with the door slightly ajar. It was very quiet and he says he could distinctly hear the precise, regular tread of Hobart's feet along the carpeted corridor. Then he heard a strangled cry of 'My God!' The next moment Hobart, white-faced and terror-stricken, had hurled himself into a chair by Purlin's side sobbing hysterically.

Purlin shook the man roughly.

"What"s the matter?" he demanded. He was deeply alarmed. Hobart was the most unlikely person to break down like this. George Purlin had seen him absolutely calm and unruffled on many an occasion when some of the Laing's parties deteriorated into violent brawls. He remembered one such brawl during which Hobart had remained quietly decanting whisky when the rest of those present had scampered all over the place at the sight of a drunken guest brandishing a knife at his adversary. It had been Hobart who walked calmly across and disarmed the man.

Hobart did not reply. He merely gulped, his eyes starting out of his head.

"Come on, man! What's the matter?" Purlin shook him again.

"The master," gasped Hobart at last. "Dead – knifed!"

Purlin felt frightened, but he seized Hobart's arm and dragged the man along with him to the bedroom. He kept his wits sufficiently about him, he said, to realise that if Hobart's news was correct, it was better to have a witness present – even a hysterical one.

The door of the bedroom stood open, just as Hobart had left it in his inglorious flight. A standard lamp, with a chromium stalk and a pleated golden-yellow shade threw its light on the bed. Purlin felt suddenly sick and his knees grew weak. Indeed it must have been a terrifying sight.

On the divan lay Samuel Laing. He was clad in a dark-blue silk dressing-gown which was open at the neck, revealing a bare chest. In the centre of that naked patch was a gaping wound on which the blood was still semi-liquid. It must have reached that stage of agglutination when it is most shiny and so reflected the light with truly macabre effect. Laing's right hand trailed on the floor. Purlin had seen plenty of dead men – and men dead from knife wounds, too, and he had no doubt that Laing was dead. But that did nothing to make the situation any less unpleasant. On the contrary, it complicated matters quite a lot.

George Purlin wanted to turn and bolt, just as Hobart had done. But he managed to keep control of himself and, probably as a relief for his own feelings, he shook Hobart once more and this time quite violently. This rough treatment appeared unnecessary. Still white-faced and a little unsteady, Hobart had now recovered his self-control. He even found time to make an apology – a point that struck very firmly in Purlin's mind.

"I'm sorry, sir," he said, "that I allowed myself to give way just now."

George Purlin grunted. "The police," he snapped. "Dial 999!"

Hobart turned and this time though he hurried it was with his accustomed dignity. Perhaps he felt that he had a reputation to recover, though I do not imagine that Purlin was in any state to be a fair critic.

It was a suspected murder case, though I don't think the word 'suspected' can have occurred to either Hobart or George Purlin. To them it was as clear a case as could be found anywhere; because it was suspected murder, therefore, the call went straight through to Central and within a minute or two Detective Inspector Richard Morris and a colleague, Sergeant Vernon Collins, were on their way to Bloomsbury.

THREE

Inspector Morris had seen knifings before. They are not altogether an uncommon sight to experienced officers of the C.I.D., especially to those who, like Dick, have served in one of the divisions in Dockland. The knife is the sailor-tough's favourite weapon – silent and very deadly in skilled hands, even when used as a missile. So Dick Morris was not at all moved when he saw the scene – at any rate it produced no such violent reactions as in Messrs Purlin and Hobart. But Dick is, all the same, a sensitive man, and I know, on his own confession, that he never sees the victim of a murder without experiencing an inward cold rage against those who hold life so cheap. For though the life that is extinguished may in itself be worthless, there are often some dependant upon it who may have to face poverty and pain through no fault of their own.

Inspector Morris waited while the divisional surgeon made his examination, which did not take long.

"Pretty obvious," said the D.S. "It's a pretty hefty wound penetrating deep – right into the arch of the aorta, I should say, which accounts for the unusually large haemorrhage. Stab wounds, as you probably know, don't bleed much as a rule. Quite fresh – been dead about an hour or so, I should say."

The Inspector nodded in agreement. He looked round

the room, after switching on the main light. His eyes narrowed as he saw a long-bladed dagger lying near the window. It was of a kind that is common in the Middle East and is a fairly regular object among the curio dealers' stock. The blade was stained with fresh blood. Inspector Morris examined the dagger without moving it. He could see that, even without the aid of powder, some fingerprints were well marked.

Samuel Laing's room was square in shape, with a heavy carpet covering only the middle, leaving in view all around highly-polished parquet blocks. French windows gave onto the balcony which ran right along the terrace of houses – common in this type of architecture. "It would be easy enough for anyone to slip along the balcony and in by those windows ..." thought the Inspector, as he beheld the scene. Suddenly he went down on his hands and knees and looked at the polished floor. It was quite unmistakable – there it was – the imprint of a bare foot, a small foot, more like a woman's. He glanced at Laing's body as it lay on the divan. Those feet were much too large to make that print and in any event Laing was wearing red leather slippers and silk socks. The print was fresh – a condensation print caused by a damp, bare foot pressing on the wax of the polish.

This was a startling discovery. Any intruder gaining access to the balcony either by climbing up a stackpipe or even through one of the corner houses would hardly have left behind a print of a bare foot. Here was certainly something that needed looking into.

After the usual routine of checking up for fingerprints, taking photographs of the body and taking stock of the room furniture, the Inspector slipped out into the road and surveyed the scene from the opposite side. It was a warm night and practically all those French windows were open. The obvious thing to do was a house-to-house call – at midnight!

Clearly, the first one to call upon was the first-floor flat next door. He walked up to the porch and inspected the neat row of brass plates. He says he could not help smiling to himself as he read: 'Miss Veronica Lloyd – first floor.' It seemed ridiculous to him to be calling at this hour and on such an errand, on my fiancée But he had no choice.

There was some delay before the bell was answered and Dick managed just in time to stop from ringing once again. Veronica herself opened the door as she had no resident servant.

"Sorry to disturb you, Veronica," he said.

She stared at him dully and gave no sign of recognition. It took Dick some time to convince her that his visit was forced upon him. Veronica, still silent, let him in but not before Sergeant Collins had joined them.

Dick admits that he was shocked by Veronica's condition. She looked to him ill and slow in comprehension, asking for almost everything to be repeated twice or even three times. This rather dull creature was certainly hardly recognizable as the bright young woman with whom he had dined, at my invitation, not so long ago, when I had been introducing Veronica to my friends.

Quietly and persistently the Inspector put his questions. What time had she come in? When had she gone to bed? Had she heard any noise along the balcony after she had retired or been disturbed at all? He confessed that he almost smiled to himself when he put that last question; he had the impression that she could barely hear him, although she was supposed to be awake.

Slowly the replies came. She had come in unusually early that night, after having dined quietly at the Narwhal. It was about nine o'clock when she had reached home and soon afterward she had gone to bed.

Dick was further told that Veronica was unused to early

retiring and she could not fall asleep for quite a long time. She certainly heard a noise – someone opening the French windows. As it was about half past ten, when Mr. Laing went for his rest, she presumed they were his windows.

So she knew Samuel Laing?

"Yes," she said, offering no explanation.

Dick had told her that Laing was dead, but either she had not understood or not heard what he was saying. At any rate she did not appear at all moved and Dick, knowing who she was, had automatically ruled her out as a suspect.

More as a police routine he had asked to see the flat.

Without a word she led the way. The flat was a mirror image of Laing's. While his bedroom was at the end of a corridor running to the right, hers was at the leftmost end of the passage. The two bedrooms were, therefore, side by side. The first shock the Inspector had was when he inspected the windows, which were standing wide open. For there, on the polished parquet blocks just inside the window, he noticed another footprint; and his photographic memory told him that it was exactly similar to the one in Laing's room. His heart skipped a beat.

He turned toward Veronica. "You do realise, Miss Lloyd," he said in a serious tone of voice, "that Mr. Laing is dead – murdered?" This time he spoke slowly and distinctly.

Veronica nodded dully. "Yes," she said, in just the same way as she had answered his question about her knowing Samuel Laing.

"Miss Lloyd," he proceeded, "you are the fiancée of a very good friend of mine. Because of that – and also because you do not seem to grasp things very clearly tonight – I am going to be quite frank with you. You are in a very serious position. A very serious position indeed," he repeated. "Mr. Laing has been murdered – stabbed to death with an Arab dagger – and there is a footprint inside his room. There is another here" – he pointed to the floor – "and I am almost certain the two are the same. Now, have you visited Samuel Laing's room tonight? You need not answer that unless you wish," he added quickly.

Veronica nodded. "Yes," she said simply.

He looked at her in astonishment.

"Miss Lloyd, do pull yourself together. Do you realise what you are saying?"

"I do." She sounded more decisive now. "Samuel Laing is dead – murdered. My footprints are in his room. I visited his room."

Looked at from whatever angle, this seemed a pretty shocking confession to Inspector Morris. He decided he had better continue his interrogation in more suitable surroundings.

"I am very sorry, Miss Lloyd," he said, "but I shall have to ask you to come along to Scotland Yard with me for some more questions. Will you dress as soon as possible? We'll wait outside the door."

"Very well," she said, and waited for the two policemen to leave her alone in her bedroom.

FOUR

Inspector Morris took Veronica to see a doctor first. He was puzzled by her state, which was quite unlike what he knew of her. But the doctor could not tell him much. All he could say was that she seemed rather shocked, as though she had been through some terrifying experience; and he warned Dick to go carefully with her. Dick nodded. Murdering a man like that would be a more than terrifying experience to most girls, he thought.

Before he questioned her again, he had some other news which disturbed him even more. As soon as they had arrived at Scotland Yard, he had asked her if she would be willing to have her fingerprints taken. She had agreed readily. The Fingerprints Department had been busy while Veronica was with the doctor, and their report was now in front of Inspector Morris. According to the experts, the fingerprints found on the hilt of the dagger were those of Veronica. The case looked almost proved.

Dick began with the dagger as soon as the questioning started. He produced it and showed it to her, having given her the usual warning, which she said she fully understood.

"Have you seen this dagger before?" he asked.

"Yes. It's mine. I bought it in a shop in King's Road, Chelsea," she replied.

His heart sank. Every word was a further knot fastened round Veronica's neck.

"What did you want with a thing like that?"

"I liked it as a curio," she answered, "but also it looked the very thing to kill someone with – someone you hated."

Mad, he thought; she must be mad. A vague echo of Lady Macbeth crossed his memory.

"This is the dagger with which Samuel Laing was killed," he said, feeling helpless in the face of a suspect who seemed set on incriminating herself up to the hilt – and Dick said that this was his actual thought and he felt like screaming at the aptness of the metaphor.

"Yes," she continued, with a dull calmness that shocked him. "I killed him. I remember now."

"Miss Lloyd," he said patiently. "I am prepared to forget that answer and give you time to think again, because I can hardly believe you realise what you are saying. You are confessing to murder."

"I know," she nodded. "But there it is. I did it. I didn't expect to get away with it and there's no need to make a fuss about things. I was done for anyway. The rope is better than the Thames. If only they don't get sentimental and refuse to hang me because I'm a woman." She had obviously forgotten that capital punishment in Britain had been abolished years ago. She can't be sane, thought Inspector Morris with compassion.

"I killed Samuel Laing because I loathed him," she went on with a sudden low-toned passion that made Dick's hair stand on end. "I hated the very air he breathed. He could only be harmless if he was dead."

Inspector Morris gave up and remembered his duty.

"You understand that I must take you into custody," he said.

"I understand, Inspector, you have to do your duty." A smile passed over her face. "I'll come quietly," she said.

And so she was arrested and taken to the cells.

Dick looked up for the first time during his explanation. His face was lined and drawn, as though he were suffering acute pain.

"I'm sorry, Mark, but there it is. There was nothing else I could do. Her confession by itself would mean nothing. I still don't understand that dull-wittedness of hers. Do you?"

"No," I replied.

"It's as clear a case on the face of it as could be," Dick went on. "There were the fingerprints – of course – which are damning. Then the footprints in both rooms. The dagger was hers on her own admission. What else could I do?"

"Nothing," I said wearily. The burden was almost too great to be borne. I felt that at any moment now I would be sure to wake up.

"Of course, there may be some hidden mistake in it all," Dick continued, though without any conviction. "What puzzles me is why Veronica hated Samuel Laing so much? Can you throw any light on that?"

I shook my head. "No. That's the question that's torturing me too," I answered.

"I'm sorry, Mark," he said weakly.

"You've nothing to be sorry about," I returned. A sudden mood of determination seized me. Veronica was in a predicament, a deep one from which there seemed no possible escape. But I must help her. Somewhere there was an explanation to all this crazy affair.

"Listen, Dick," I continued, "I shall act for Veronica. In the first place, she's my fiancée. In the second, she has, so far as I know, no relatives or friends to help her and look after her interests. In the third, I'm a doctor and it looks as though there's something queer about her condition. Can I see her – alone?"

Dick cupped his chin in his hands. "Yes. I think I can fix that," he replied, after a thoughtful pause.

"And can I, as an interested party, see the dagger and the room and all the rest?"

"That'll be more difficult," he said, "but I'll do my best. You'd better be here about ten tomorrow and then I'll take you to see her."

"Thanks."

I got to my feet. The room circled round me. I could no longer remember anything but that Veronica was in a terrible, tragic situation and I was helpless. My world had disappeared. Then I became aware of strong arms supporting me and Dick's solicitous voice talking to me.

"Steady, old man – steady. You'd better go home. I'll get a car to take you back and one of my men will bring yours in the morning – or you can come here by taxi and drive back yourself if you're fit."

I nodded. I didn't care about my car. They could throw it in the Thames so far as I was concerned. But they took me home and when we arrived I could not even remember where I kept my latch-key. They woke up old Maggie and gave her instructions to put me to bed. For myself I had just sufficient wits about me to give myself a dose of potassium bromide and tell Maggie to make sure I was at Scotland Yard by ten in the morning.

"I'll wake you, Master Mark," I heard Maggie's voice and then the world went blank again and I was sinking through an endless vertical tunnel with slippery sides so that I could do nothing to arrest my descent.

I spent the night alternating between periods of oblivion and fits of utter sleeplessness. Several times I awoke with a start thinking it was time to get ready for my visit to Scotland Yard, only to find it was barely an hour since I had previously looked at my watch. I did not dream. My wakeful moments were the perpetual nightmare; the moments of sleep were the periods of sanity.

When the housekeeper called me, I felt shaky and utterly depressed.

"Steady, Doctor Mark," a voice startled me. "Get dressed or you'll be late for your appointment." Maggie's eyes were moist with tears.

"Thank you, Maggie," I said and went into the bathroom to shave. Later, when I had bathed and dressed, I felt a little better, though the breakfast that Maggie had prepared for me I felt unable to eat. I just gulped a cup of hot tea and hurried to the street. I hailed a passing taxi and told the driver to take me to Scotland Yard.

Inspector Morris was waiting for me. "Good morning, Mark," he greeted me. "I'm afraid I have nothing to cheer you up with. This is one of the few times that I wish I could be proved wrong."

"The impossible sometimes happens," I said without much conviction.

"I wish I could share your view," he returned.

"Can I see Veronica?"

"In a little while," he answered. "She's being brought up here and you can see her alone. It's a hell of a concession in a murder charge, you do realise that?"

"Yes, I do Dick. I'm very grateful to you."

"Sit down a minute, Mark," he said. "I must tell you something more before you see Veronica."

I sank into a chair. "Something new?"

He nodded. "Yes."

After offering me a cigarette and lighting one for himself, he sat back and sighed slightly.

"Early this morning," he began, "Veronica sent up a message saying she wanted to make a statement – but only to me personally. So I went down." He paused. "Mark," he went on softly, "I don't think you know anything about this.

It might be a shock to you, but I think you ought to hear me out before you see Veronica. As a matter of fact, it was Veronica herself who insisted that I should tell you. You see, she thinks you may not want to see her when you hear her confession."

"It can hardly be worse than what's happened already."

"In one way – no. But then you didn't know – neither did I – the revelations she made clear in her confession."

"I see. But for God's sake let's hear it."

This is what Inspector Morris told me:

Samuel Laing was the type of man who always kept just on the right side of the law in spite of his various shady deals. He had begun as a bookmaker and had also interests in quite a few gambling clubs. Some years ago, he had also acquired an interest in a small group of magazines. It was here that Veronica met him. Like so many of his kind, he had a taste for women and no doubt Veronica attracted him from the first. She applied for a job on one of his papers and got it – at a price! She was just beginning then as a journalist and she thought it a grand opportunity. Inexperienced, she did not know what was in store for her.

Samuel Laing was a man of great cunning which had brought him success in business as well as in his affairs with women. Veronica was flattered by his obvious interest, as many other young girls in similar circumstances would have been. He dined with her several times and although one or two people dropped warning hints to her, she did not heed them. With the confidence of youth, she thought she could deal with any situation. And Laing behaved like the perfect gentleman, thus winning her trust.

Veronica was going through a hard time then. I had heard something of it before, but she always preferred to be silent as far as her past was concerned and I respected her attitude. Her only surviving relative was her mother, a chronic invalid, whose small funds were far from sufficient. The burden of supporting both of them fell on Veronica's shoulders. She managed somehow, but often was forced to borrow money which she could not repay.

Samuel Laing was very sympathetic and understanding. He insisted upon helping her financially and paid off all outstanding debts. Her gratitude had no bounds and the inevitable was bound to happen. Laing won another of his victories. Veronica became his mistress.

For some reason or other Laing seems to have formed a particularly strong possessive feeling for her. He did not discard her or get tired of her as he usually did with his other women. Quite the opposite, and when Veronica began to wake up to her hopeless position, wishing to end their relationship, he did not hesitate to point out to her the alternative of dismissal from her job. She had attained some sort of a position now and was accepted as a society correspondent. All this could be ruined if Laing put his threats into execution, as he said he would should Veronica leave him.

So it went on. She felt herself powerless to escape, and every day the liaison was protracted, the weaker her will to get free of him became. But at last the break was made. Samuel Laing appeared to tire of her. Her mother died and that gave her greater freedom. Laing, too, was prepared to let her go if she resigned her position as the permanent correspondent of his magazines. She agreed to that readily.

Everything looked bright for her again. For the first time in her life she found her work an absorbing pleasure. She made rapid progress, acquired sufficient connections to set up as an independent freelance artist-journalist. But she made one mistake: she remained in the flat in which Laing had originally installed her. It had that convenient balcony giving them mutual access to each other's rooms.

For a while, following the end of their liaison, Laing seemed to have left her in peace. It was during this period that we two met and not too long after became engaged. The news reached Samuel Laing, as it could hardly fail to do. The engagement was unfortunately widely reported in the gossip columns at the time, perhaps by Veronica's journalist friends.

Jealousy, or perhaps injured pride, made Samuel Laing change his mind. He decided he wanted Veronica back and he told her so, but she refused him bluntly. She felt free and safe now and continued to rebuff him in no uncertain way. She told him outright that she hated him and did not want to see him ever.

Veronica, however, had not reckoned with his cunning. He was not a man to be put aside that lightly. He told her that she was a woman with a past – not an ideal wife for a Harley Street specialist. She still stood firm. He told her in great detail precisely what he proposed to do in the way of spreading a whispering campaign against me. The gossip that she was one of Samuel Laing's cast-off women would hardly help me in my career.

Veronica became frantic. The thought of losing the man she really loved with all her heart terrified her. She felt completely lost. She did not know what to do. If she still refused him, the threat against me would be put into effect; if she surrendered, she would have to give me up. Samuel Laing gave her a week to think it over. He died on the night of Thursday, 7th September.

Veronica's week of grace expired on Friday, 8th September.

FIVE

Inspector Morris paused for a moment. "Not a very nice story," he commented, "but that's what Veronica told me. Filthy swine – that Samuel Laing!" he added bitterly.

For a little while I remained silent. It was a sordid enough tale and it was almost incredible that Veronica should be the principal actress in it. I pride myself upon being a liberal-minded man, but all the same, I have to confess that a feeling of slight nausea passed through me as the details came out. This feeling, however, lasted but briefly and was replaced by a yearning to be by Veronica's side. The original impression that the whole thing was an elaborately dressed nightmare returned to me.

"If Veronica did it – I still say IF – she did an act of social justice," I said grimly. "When can I see her?"

Dick looked at his watch. "She's due now and we'll be told the moment she arrives. Perhaps, as a human being, I agree with you, Mark, but as a police officer I know that the worth or otherwise of the murdered person doesn't count. And this, Mark, gets blacker and blacker."

"But surely, an English jury – any jury – wouldn't convict in such circumstances?"

Inspector Morris shook his head. "They would have no choice at all. The murder was obviously deliberate and the outcome of forethought on her own confession."

"What about the so-called 'Crime passionel'?"

"That is the French definition of a certain kind of murder. Unfortunately the English law does not recognize such a variety of murder."

"There's no doubt that her dagger was the weapon?" I asked, clutching wildly at another of the frailest straws.

"How could there be?" He shrugged. "The blade was covered with Laing's blood and the hilt had Veronica's fingerprints. No judge can tell a jury anything else."

"I suppose so," I said, and there was silence. Both of us relapsed into thought.

"Poor Veronica!" I thought, and a hundred and one little details came back to me with unexpected vividness. I remembered how reluctant she had been to talk of her past and how I felt hurt at times, though I had never tried to break into her reticence. I knew a little of her unhappy youth and of her struggle to help her dying mother. I recalled, too, how often she had seemed to be brooding and then come to the point of saying something. Now I came to think of it, in the light of what I heard, I seemed to feel her appealing mutely to me for help that I could not give because I did not know her need.

Now I knew. It was ghastly, terrible. But she was wrong if she thought it would shake my trust and belief in her or alter my love for her. Veronica needed my help and protection now more desperately than she had ever done or would ever again. If I had not been able to realise the mental anguish she was in, I could have found it in me to resent a little that evidence of lack of faith. It was not for me to cast the first stone, even if I would.

My reverie was interrupted by the buzz of the telephone. Dick spoke in it briefly and then looked at me with a slight nod.

"She's here, Mark. You'd better go to her at once. I'll give you as long as I can, but I can't stretch regulations endlessly.

You must make it snappy. I'll show you the way."

I was on my feet in an instant.

Veronica was alone. The wardress was standing outside the door as we came along the passage and smiled sympathetically at me as I passed. Dick left me at the entrance.

"Mark!" She half moved towards me and then stopped short, as though stricken with sudden, tormenting doubts.

"Veronica – darling!" I cried and took her in my arms. So for a short space we enjoyed that intimate communion of silence which is more eloquent than words to lovers. But after a little while I released myself gently and pressed her down into the hard wooden chair with which the room was furnished, while I perched on the table holding her hand.

"Did Inspector Morris tell you – everything?" she asked, suddenly dropping her eyes.

"Yes."

"And you still want me?" There was almost a note of surprise in her voice.

"Of course, darling." I shrugged my shoulders miserably. "Surely you must have known that if you'd told me we could have found a way out together."

She squeezed my hand and looked deep into my eyes. It meant more to me than any flow of words.

There was still silence, but I roused myself with an effort. "Darling Veronica, we've got very little time together. It's a special privilege that they've allowed this interview at all. We've a lot to talk about."

"There's not much to say, is there?" The resignation in her voice appalled me.

"But all this is utterly incredible," I exclaimed. "Are you really serious when you say you killed Laing?"

She shuddered slightly, but kept her self-control.

"I must have," she answered.

I looked up sharply. "What do you mean – 'you must have'?"

"Well, Mark, you see, I planned it – though not quite like that – and it happened. You see, I knew I was helpless – oh! how I wish I had told you now! – so when I saw that dagger I thought I'd buy it – for emergencies. I thought – I knew – I'd have to give in, and then – then," she shuddered again, more markedly – "he'd come creeping in through the open window as he used to do." She flushed. "And then I thought that when he got close enough I'd drive the dagger into him."

"But he didn't come, did he?"

"No. I got mixed in the dates, I suppose. I was nearly out of my mind those last few days. That was why I didn't want to see you yesterday. No, he didn't come and I must have gone into his room and killed him."

I looked at her keenly. I felt she was holding something back.

"Veronica," I said slowly, "for God's sake be frank with me. You're holding something back."

She lifted her head and looked me full in the eyes and then she relapsed into thought for a few moments.

"Yes," she said at last. "I can tell you, dear, but it doesn't help. It's something I've been meaning to ask you about for some time. Ever since I was a kid I've had a habit of walking in my sleep. It happens when I'm worried and this past week – well, once I woke up and found myself in the outside corridor." She paused again. "I must have been in his room."

"You mean that you killed Samuel Laing in your sleep? Do you remember going to his room?"

She shook her head. "No, I don't remember but I've a memory of something. It seems to me that some time during that night I picked up the dagger and took it out of the sheath and thought how useful it was going to be." She paused. "That's all I remember. But when Inspector Morris came and told me that Samuel had been killed, I seemed to know at once all about it. That often happens after I've walked in my sleep."

I did not reply immediately.

"And you had that feeling about this murder?"

"Yes. Besides I was numbed and shocked when Inspector Morris saw me, just as I always felt I should be if I did it."

"My God! You should have told me about this before!" I said. "I could have helped you." What Veronica was describing were the symptoms of a recognized form of somnambulism, which I had met in my practice on a good few occasions. "And you should have told Dick. This puts an entirely fresh complexion on the affair. If it happened like that, you really know nothing about it and no doubt that could be a defence."

Veronica looked at me for a long while. "And that means, I suppose, a verdict of 'Guilty but insane', and being sentenced to be detained during the Queen's pleasure? Mark," she went on, looking at me with large, appealing eyes, "I know you want to help me, but do you think that the mere exchanging of a life sentence for one of 'detention during Her Majesty's pleasure' would help me? Knowing you're perfectly sane yet treated as a lunatic for God knows how many years! Could anything be more ghastly?"

I nodded slowly. The prospect was far from alluring.

"As soon as I was told of Laing's death, I knew I must have killed him in my sleep. That's the long and short of it. So the only thing to do was to confess. Please don't try to help me to be sentenced as a criminal lunatic."

Tears stood in her eyes, though her face remained calm.

"Very well, darling," I replied at length. "But for all that

I think this is something Dick ought to know. We owe him that much for all the consideration he has given us."

There was a knock at the door.

"Will you finish now, sir?" said the voice of the wardress.

"Just a few more moments, please," I replied. "We must get the best lawyers available to handle your case. I'll see to that. Promise me, darling, that you'll not lose hope."

"The only hope I have is to see this ghastly business ended as soon as possible." She looked at me pleadingly. "I feel happier knowing that you still love me. That's all that matters." She flung her arms about me and wept into my shoulder ...

Veronica crying with her head on my shoulder ... How long ago was it? It seemed ages to me and how different were her tears then ...

It was during my last summer holidays. Originally I intended to fly to the Greek Islands but changed my mind when I found that Veronica was going to Venice to cover the Film Festival for an illustrated magazine.

"How lovely," I exclaimed. "I'll come too!"

"But didn't you want to explore the romantic Greek Islands?" she smiled.

"They can wait," I smiled back. "But to be with you and in Venice – how can the Greek Islands compete?"

"Yes, it's wonderful that we'll be together. I'll arrange with the editor for a longer holiday. How long can you stay, Mark?"

"Only two weeks, I'm afraid. It's all that the hospital authorities can give me."

"How heavenly – two weeks in Venice! ..." She looked at me in silence as if to find out how much I really wanted to be with her.

The first night, I took Veronica for dinner in a restaurant

on the Grand Canal. She wore a plain light blue dress that reflected the blue waters of the lagoon and contrasted beautifully with her light blonde hair, falling like gentle waves on her shoulders. I looked into her eyes. "Thank you, Veronica, thank you for everything."

"For what, Mark?" She pretended not to understand.

"For being with me, here in Venice. For making my holiday memorable."

"It's only the first day, Mark." Her soft laughter glided over the water and lost itself in the sound of splashing waves on ancient stone walls. "You might change your mind." She laughed again.

I ignored her making fun of me. "Yes, it's only the beginning ..."

Envious eyes followed us as we entered the restaurant and were led by the waiter to a side-table overlooking the lagoon.

Veronica smiled at me. "What's needed now is soft music to complete the evening," she said as she sipped gently of the cold champagne she held in her hand.

As if by magic, a trio of itinerary musicians appeared on the floor and after looking around for a moment, selected our table for their serenade.

"They must have guessed that you're an important man." Veronica smiled again.

"They're not bothering about me," I said. "It's to your beauty that they're paying homage." I lifted my glass. "I join with them – to beauty! To you, Veronica!"

"Thank you, Mark," she said, moved.

I paid the bill and after leaving a generous tip to the musicians, we walked hand in hand out into the fresh, salty air. The peculiar smell – so typical of Venice – filled our nostrils as we strolled along the Canal into the open square of San Marco Cathedral.

"Shall we walk around and see some of the old palaces?"

Veronica nodded in silence and came closer to me, squeezing my arm tenderly.

The night was warm and still. Only the sound of the gondoliers' voices inviting passers-by to their gondolas disturbed the stillness.

"Shall we?"

"Oh, yes, Mark, let's take one!" She laughed like a child. "I'm mad about gondolas."

"Only about gondolas?" I feigned sadness.

"No, not only about gondolas." She pressed my hand.

The gondola glided gently along the Canal into the open lagoon. We saw the moon's reflection mingling with ours in the waters. We sat on the bottom of the gondola close to each other with our arms intertwined.

"Mark?" she asked softly, turning her face to me. "Do you love me?"

I did not answer. I simply kissed her gently and held my lips pressed on hers for a while. No words were necessary to tell her of my loneliness before I met her. In that one kiss all my desire and plans for the two of us were expressed and she understood. She put her arms round my neck and held me for a few more seconds.

"It's getting chilly, darling. Let's go back to the hotel."

We were silent for the rest of the voyage and walked silently to the hotel. Slowly we climbed to the second floor where our rooms were situated.

"Mark," she said while fumbling for her key in her handbag. "It's not going to be a week-end romance, is it? I don't like week-end romances. I'm not made for them." She held my eyes in her steady gaze. "I really hope that this one is for keeps – otherwise I couldn't get so involved. I'm not just trying to kill time – you do know what I mean, don't you?"

I gripped her hand and held her gaze.

"I don't like week-end romances either, Veronica." I let go of her hand and took out the small box with the solitary-diamond ring that I had bought that afternoon.

"Let's see if it fits," I smiled. "Which is the engagement finger? The left one?"

"No, the right one," she answered simply. "How beautiful! Thank you, Mark. Thank you again." She slipped the ring onto her trembling finger.

"I want you, Veronica!"

"I want you, too," she answered quietly. "Give me a few moments." She unlocked the door of her room and went in silently.

I went back to my room to undress. Pouring myself a small whisky and soda I sat for a few seconds in the armchair near the window. Quietly I retraced my steps into Veronica's room.

She was lying in her bed covered up to her neck. Her moist eyes looked up at me. "Mark, do you mind if I switch off the light? I feel a little embarrassed."

"No, darling. I don't mind." I smiled and started to take off the top of my pyjamas. The moonlight shone through the open window. I knelt beside her bed and lifted the sheet from her breasts. Then I put my arms around her warm, trembling body and kissed her.

Still trembling, she opened her arms and wound them round my neck. "Oh, Mark, Mark darling!"

I unfolded my arms and threw back the sheet that was still covering the rest of her body. I raised my head and greedily beheld the wonderful naked creature now lying calmly on the bed. The moonlight made her look almost unreal.

For a moment neither of us spoke. Then she asked gently: "Mark, am I beautiful? I mean am I beautiful enough for you to love me for always?"

"Oh yes, yes!" I said. "You're beautiful enough for all the world to love you but I want you only for myself, my darling." Her firm, shapely breasts heaved evenly like gentle waves spreading ripples down to her body and stopping at her thin waist. Only her long legs and strong, beautifully outlined thighs were still and vigorous as if to suppress the inner desire that shook her body.

"I must be beautiful always for you." Her voice broke the spell, disturbing the silence of the moonlight.

"You will be beautiful for me as long as you live," I answered kissing her lips.

All my passion for her, repressed for so long, came flooding like a bush-fire over me. I kissed her breasts over and over again, then her lips once more, feeling her warmth enwrapping me and holding me as in a trance. Then we made love and it was more exciting than anything I had ever known, a wild primitive love that shook us both.

Veronica lay in my arms all night, holding me close, happier, she said, than she had ever dreamed was possible. I kissed her again and made love to her once more, growing bolder as we became more intimate until, both spent, we fell asleep in each other's arms somewhere around dawn.

That day Veronica was a changed girl. Whereas she had been perhaps a little proud and off-putting in her manner, now she was humble, servile towards me almost. She would take my hand and brush it against her mouth. Her eyes would look into mine with such devotion and gratitude that I too felt humble and more glad to be alive than ever before.

Often I would see tears running down Veronica's cheeks and I knew that these were not bitter tears of pain or despair. They were, she said again and again, while I dried her cheeks, tears that had to come out of her system. They were tears of joy and happiness, and I did not ask why?

Because I too was happy and enjoying our prospect of a life together.

There was another knock at the door and Veronica tore herself from me. Before the door was fully opened she had recovered her calm, but as they led her away she turned one look on me. It was like a last farewell. I felt she was trying to express in that look all the love she had ever had for me and the gratitude she felt for our happy hours together. And then she was gone. I turned away, my head sunk on my breast. Yes, I confess it, I nearly broke down in front of a policeman waiting to lead me back to Inspector Morris's room. And if I had, would it really have been so much to my discredit?

SIX

Inspector Morris was not in the superintendent's office when I returned to it. The room was empty and to pass time I dropped into a chair and settled down to wait. I thought of Veronica as they had taken her from me. Surely that lovely girl was not, could not be a killer! And her confession to me that she thought she must have killed Samuel Laing in her sleep-walking was going round and round in my mind. My head began to reel and I was in the very depths of despair when Dick came back. He cast a sympathetic look at me.

"You're taking it badly, Mark," he said quietly. "I almost feel that way myself. I'm going to take you out and give you a drink before lunch. We both need it and I feel damned hungry – and tired, too. I've been at it for over fifteen hours now, apart from a catnap on a wooden chair."

"That's O.K. with me. I don't feel very hungry but I do certainly need that drink. Let's go!"

After I had been fortified by a couple of double Scotches, I suggested a restaurant where I am well known and could get a table almost immediately.

We both ate our food in silence and then during our pause for coffee to be served, Dick looked at me.

"Well?" he asked. "Have you nothing to say?"

I returned his glance firmly. "Yes, Dick, I have something to say."

"Go on, man. Let's hear it!"

"Veronica told me the whole truth today. I think you should know it."

"The whole truth?" Dick looked rather surprised. "You mean to say there's something fresh?"

"In a way."

"She doesn't deny the confession, I suppose?"

"No. She sticks by that. Dick," I went on seriously, "Veronica is convinced she killed Samuel Laing, but the way she told me she killed him is what bothers me."

"What way, Mark?"

Briefly I told him what Veronica had confessed to me, and of her attitude towards her position. Dick nodded gravely.

"I respect and understand her, Mark," he said sincerely. "But if anything on the sleep-walking lines is put up at this stage, it will look like an ingenious attempt to wriggle out of a very nasty hole, however true it may be. Any judge would point that out to a jury and tell them to trust their own common sense. I can just imagine it," he went on cynically.

"I suppose you're right."

"I'm afraid I am, Mark," he replied, finishing his coffee. "Cut that out of your mind. It looks to me, my friend, as if the only thing to do is to respect Veronica's wishes and hope that a sentence of life imprisonment *is* carried out."

I stared at him with open mouth. I am sure I went white. Here was Dick, my friend Dick, the one detective officer in Scotland Yard whose judgement I entirely trusted, virtually condemning my fiancée, my lovely Veronica to something worse than death! But I felt no rage. I knew that it was only honesty that was speaking.

I signed to the waiter for my bill.

From Scotland Yard, they took Veronica to the police court. Only formal evidence of arrest was given, and she was remanded for a week. That afternoon I saw Betterdale, a solicitor friend of mine, who put me in touch with a firm specializing in criminal matters. Whatever the outcome, however black the case was, Veronica should not want for the best defence that money could provide.

The few days that followed Veronica's formal arrest were a nightmare for me. I told Miss Hughes, my secretary, that I would not be in for at least a week and that any future appointments should be deferred. Then I asked for a week's leave of absence from the hospital authorities and was lucky to receive it without any troubles.

Inspector Morris was exceptionally good to me. He kept me informed, in defiance of most of the regulations, of every development. There was nothing new, however, with the exception that more details came to light about Samuel Laing. The man was an utter scoundrel, but he was clever and managed to keep on the right side of the law. Even though the police now had access to all his papers, they could find nothing on which they might have taken action.

What hurt most was the detail about Samuel Laing's manifold intrigues. He was never content with one woman at a time and it was a depressing and humiliating thought that Veronica had been merely one of many. To me it was all quite nauseating. The more I heard about him, the more rage surged up in me that Veronica was almost certain to suffer for wiping this lecher from the face of the earth. It was utterly unjust and unfair. But, as Assize judges have frequently remarked, criminal courts are not courts of morals. Yet with each new revelation, I grew more and more determined that whether Veronica was technically guilty of murder or not, she should not be made to suffer life imprisonment.

"It's almost like one of those detective novels," said Dick to me one evening, when he called at my home. "From what my men have turned up, Veronica wasn't the only one by a long shot with the wish to bump off Samuel Laing. There were literally dozens of people with a motive to murder this man. Unfortunately for her, Veronica got in first."

Inspector Morris always spoke now as though Veronica's guilt was beyond the remotest doubt. I did not argue with him. He pitied me, I think, for what he thought was my ridiculous persistence in trying to find a way out.

"Yes," Dick went on casually, "Laing even had anonymous letters threatening his life. We've found five such letters, but they are useless to us in the circumstances."

I did not comment on this. It only increased my bitterness. No one ought to go to prison for killing Samuel Laing; but if Fate decreed that someone had to, I had much rather it were someone other than Veronica. It was an uncharitable thought, I admit, but then I loved Veronica.

The next day I went to see the solicitor who had been acting for Veronica, a youngish man who had been concerned with the defence in many recent criminal trials. The only regret he had, so he informed me, was that in Veronica's case there was so little to be done for the defence.

All my determination was needed to prevail upon him to see Sir Gilbert Howes, Q.C. – an outstanding criminal counsel. It was the result of Vanlien's interview with Sir Gilbert that I was to hear that day.

Vanlien – he was of Dutch extraction several generations back – did not waste words in polite exchanges. "I have seen Sir Gilbert," he said almost as soon as I had sat down, "and his opinion, I'm afraid, is exactly what I expected and warned you about."

"You mean he declines to accept the brief?" I asked.

"Not exactly that. But his view is that there is no case for the defence at all. He could recommend Miss Lloyd to plead guilty. I think he feels – though he doesn't put it that way –

that it would be sheer waste of his time – and, incidentally, of your money. One of the sound juniors, like Benchwood, for example, could do as well as Sir Gilbert. That is to protect the interests of Miss Lloyd in court as much as possible."

"That doesn't sound at all hopeful," I remarked glumly.

He spread his hands. "No," he said, "but how can you be hopeful?" And again he went through the case against Veronica as Dick had done, but with a greater wealth of argument and explanation. "Frankly, Doctor Harding," he concluded, "I think you are being a little unreasonable in persisting in your belief that a plausible defence can be made. I can assure you that if you are dissatisfied with what I have done, I have no objection to handing over the case to other advisers of your choice."

I hastened to reassure him that I quite saw his point of view and was more than satisfied with his work. "It is also the point of view of Inspector Morris," I concluded. "If you would rather I took other advice ..."

"No, no," he put in hastily. "I can sympathize entirely with your attitude, of course. But there are facts that cannot be got round or explained away. In your profession, doctor, as in mine, you cannot blink at facts."

"That is true. Sometimes, though, you misinterpret facts or are even quite mistaken in them."

"I wish I could think that either of those contingencies operated in this case," he said.

I left him feeling that the unanimous opinion was that I was a blind fool who refused to see things as they were because my eyes were clouded with sentiment. No doubt that was true to a certain extent. But like our Johnny, who was the only one in step, I could almost feel that I was right and that all the others were wrong. For I was the only one who knew Veronica intimately; all the rest, even Inspector Morris, who knew her personally, were strangers. They looked at the facts that the police discovered. But they all ignored the most important thing in the whole business: Veronica's personality. To me it was utterly unbelievable that she could have committed murder.

I had tried to put this argument to Inspector Morris, but though he admitted that personality was an important factor, he could not agree that my estimate of Veronica's potentialities for murder was correct or that it could play any decisive part in this particular case. There was no malice in his argument. He was, I think, trying to help me to see the light of truth.

"Can't you see, Mark," he was arguing, "you couldn't begin to prove your opinion was right in a court. Putting all else aside, there is one thing – one damning thing – against it."

"You mean her confession about buying the dagger, I suppose. A lot of people have thought of murder but could never commit one or even make the arrangements for it. I expect I have myself."

"I've certainly wanted to murder some people," Inspector Morris had replied. "I admit that. But not to the point of buying a weapon for the purpose. Come along, Mark. You're doing yourself a lot of harm by clinging so obstinately to this belief in Veronica's innocence. It'll make the end so much harder when it comes – as I'm afraid it will."

"I don't think so, even now."

"You're just being obstinate and it isn't like you," he had said. "It does you credit as a man but it won't enhance your reputation as a clear thinker."

"Perhaps you're right, Dick. But there it is, my friend, I love Veronica – now more than ever. Oh, God! There must be some way out! There has to be!"

"I'm sorry, really very sorry for you, Mark." He had put his hand on my shoulder. "But believe me, you'll never convince a British judge and a British jury that a psychologist's opinion of a personality is of more importance than tangible things like fingerprints and blood-stained daggers and a very powerful motive to back them up. It doesn't make sense, Mark, and you'd be the first to admit it if you weren't so prejudiced, as you have every reason to be."

There we had left it.

SEVEN

The defence had, of course, been reserved, and Veronica had been committed for trial. I was not surprised when Vanlien told me that Sir Gilbert Howes, Q.C. had declined the brief 'with regrets'. The reason behind it all was only too clear. No one believed in Veronica's innocence. Even Veronica asserted that she was guilty and the more I argued with her – I was courteously allowed a number of interviews with her – the more she hardened in her opinion that I was wasting my time and showing a loyalty that was very touching but pointless.

I was, it seemed, the only person who did not take a verdict of guilty as a foregone conclusion. For I did go as far as that – not only did I insist that Veronica was innocent, but I maintained that it should be possible to prove her innocence. She, above all, scoffed at the idea.

"Darling," she said to me, "you're very sweet, I know, and you do love me still for which I'm grateful, but really you're behaving like a lunatic. I did it. I may not remember the actual details, but I'm as certain as I'm standing here that I pushed that dagger into him. Why must you get this idea into your head that I didn't?"

"Because the idea of your committing murder is just plain nuts," I replied inelegantly.

She shrugged her pretty shoulders at me. "Nuts or not,"

cried Veronica, "I did murder him in my sleep and that's that."

"Well, let's admit that," I returned. "Why hush it up? You weren't responsible for your actions and therefore you can't be proved guilty of the crime."

"Perhaps not." Her voice was scornful. "But in that case I'm certified and carted off to the asylum. Oh, Mark, don't let's go over all that again. You're only making things worse for me, you know. If you love me as you say, then please let things take their course!" Tears ran down her cheeks which she did not try to hide.

From that last interview I came away with an increased feeling of hopelessness. Whichever way I turned I seemed to ram by head against a solid wall.

The time of the trial drew nearer, but still there seemed no way out. Almost every night I awoke with the terrible picture of Veronica being sentenced to life imprisonment before me. There was Veronica, my poor lovely Veronica, standing in the dock; there was the judge with the black cap on his head. The room seemed to reverberate with his dread words – 'sentenced to life imprisonment'. The dream was so real that I would find myself ready to cry out in my anguish.

Then I asked myself again and again what would happen to me? There would be nothing to live for if Veronica should go. Curiously I found myself with one overriding wish – that the prison walls which would surround Veronica's remaining years should also embrace mine, so that we might share together a life so different from the one we had planned before her arrest. It was a grim and fantastic desire. I knew it to be quite impossible of realization. But surely, if Veronica was put away for life, there was no reason why I should not go the same way. After all, there were quite a number of people whose removal would benefit the world and I would not be at all unwilling to be the cleansing agent.

Irresistibly, my thoughts turned to considering whom I should choose as my victim, the method I should use and the details of the crime …

If Inspector Richard Morris could have looked into my secret thoughts then he would have had a terrible shock. But he did not. My thoughts on that subject at least were my own. I would share them with no one. But my behaviour had all the symptoms of a guilt complex. Because I could not save Veronica I was identifying myself with my victim and trying to expiate my own guilt by sharing her fate mentally. This conclusion came to me as a profound shock, but it did me good. It brought me back to more practical affairs. I had to do something. If I did not, the guilt feeling would increase and disaster would follow. The plain lesson was that it was no good mooning about the place giving way to substitute fantasies. I was getting as bad as any of the neurotics who found their way to my consulting rooms, for me – me, of all people! – to put right. I was trying to make fantasies the substitute for action – difficult action that seemed impossible of attainment.

The more I saw the need for drastic and immediate action, the less I could find to do. I thought of everything. I built up the most elaborate hypothesis, but the superstructure became almost at once too heavy for the foundations and the whole thing quickly collapsed. There were moments when, worn out mentally, I was on the verge of confessing that I was wrong and that Veronica was guilty. But always the picture of Veronica as I knew her rose clearly before my eyes. It was impossible. The most I could admit was that she had killed Samuel Laing in a somnambulistic state, so that she was actually, if not morally, guilty. That alone was terrible enough, but it seemed the inevitable conclusion to reach. It was the one thing that must not be mentioned, for though it might save Veronica from life imprisonment, it would lead her to something worse. 'Detained during Her Majesty's pleasure!' What fate, indeed, could be more ghastly for a woman like Veronica who was as sane as I was – perhaps, at this time, even saner!

A few days before the trial I had an interview with Vanlien and the counsel who was appearing for Veronica. Guy Manville Hereward was one of the brightest rising stars of the Bar, a man for whom high distinction was inevitable.

I was still as far from finding a solution to my problems as ever when I entered Vanlien's office. He and Hereward greeted me politely – Hereward, in fact, almost cordially – but there was a chilly atmosphere. At last Vanlien spoke, slowly, deliberately, almost reluctantly.

"Hereward wants to make quite sure that you fully understand the position," he said. "That's why I've asked you to call here."

"I think I understand it only too well and all of you think the case is hopeless." I spoke bitterly, looking at Hereward. His eyes met mine and I felt somehow that a bond of friendship had been suddenly formed between us.

Guy Hereward – a pleasant-looking man with a crisp but friendly voice – smiled at me.

"Yes, I wanted to talk to you, Harding," he said. "I see I can speak quite openly, for you don't appear to be under any illusions. I'm not saying that the position is quite as you put it. The whole thing turns on how we interpret that word hopeless. If you mean that a verdict of 'guilty' is a probability, I agree with it. But if you mean – well, that Miss Lloyd is as good as sentenced for life, I don't agree."

I looked at him. He nodded slightly and continued.

"The case is just a little too watertight – or should I say airtight? An American lawyer looking at all the facts would find them so remarkable that he'd suspect a first-class police frame-up and act accordingly. However," he smiled ironically, "this isn't America, and, of course, our police wouldn't dream of a frame-up."

Startled at his air of scepticism I jerked upright. "Do you doubt the evidence, then?" I asked quickly.

He shook his head. "No. I'm only looking at it from the outside. But you, Harding, say you're the only one who doesn't regard the case as hopeless. What are your grounds? Do *you* doubt the evidence?"

I shook my head in turn. "No. I wish I could. Veronica herself doesn't deny the facts, but I base my belief – my conviction, really, on the character and personality of Veronica."

To my surprise Hereward nodded sympathetically. "Yes," he said softly. "That has been in my mind too, from the very first time I met Miss Lloyd. It's a strange tangle. There are the facts, and there's no getting round them. Yet my feeling is that they and the person don't match up. You know what I mean. The impression I got is that the crime was forced upon her by circumstances she wasn't strong enough to resist, or perhaps at that moment was too upset mentally to consider coldly and rationally."

"Go on," I said eagerly. A ray of hope was dawning on me. Here was someone who at least was prepared to go some of the way with me.

He smiled at me indulgently. Perhaps my eagerness was a little naive.

"Unfortunately I can't detect anything of that sort about Miss Lloyd," he resumed. "I have rarely met a young woman who had her head screwed on so absolutely in the right way. But I found something else," he said with emphasis. "I believe that Miss Lloyd is holding something back. She doesn't deny the facts but she can't offer much, even for my private ear, by way of confirmation. Harding," he said seriously, "Miss Lloyd is your fiancée, and your loyalty towards her can only spring from a very deep affection and love for her. I'm here to defend her to the best of my ability and I beg of you if you know anything that I don't, please tell me. It is a disservice to her – and to me and Vanlien here – to hide anything, no matter how trivial."

I was staggered by the acuteness of his perception. But what was I to do? I had the image of Veronica pleading to me not to do or say anything that would make her 'guilty but insane'.

Hereward was talking again, and his words broke sharply into my thoughts.

"Perhaps I had better be more precise," he was saying. "I can get from Miss Lloyd no satisfactory account of how she is supposed to have committed the crime. There is a very nasty gap in the story. It may or may not sound incredible to you" – he raised his head suddenly and gave me a sharp look – "but it is as though her story was made to fit the facts of the fingerprints and so on and she is not prepared to go further than necessary beyond the bare essentials of consistency. No, my friend, I feel Miss Lloyd is hiding something and I must know the truth one way or the other."

There was something very like an accusation here that Veronica and I were misleading him by suppressing facts. I thought quickly. There was only one thing to do and that was to tell this keen-minded man the whole story.

"Thank you, Hereward," I said slowly. "You have been frank with me and I appreciate it. The only way in which I can repay your frankness is to be equally frank with you."

He bowed slightly. "Thank you," he said sharply.

"You see," I went on, "you have come very near to the truth. Veronica knows nothing about the murder, and her story is, as you put it, made to fit the facts. I'll tell you now the truth as she and I believe it to be."

He listened with the utmost attention as I gave him the explanation in terms of somnambulism. Once or twice he nodded as though the story did not come as a complete surprise to him. When I had finished he sat back in his chair and remained for a while in reflective silence.

"Thank you, Harding," said Hereward at last. "I find that story much more credible than the one I have had up till now. It's a pity I've got to know it so late, but there's still a little time to do something. Would it be indiscreet to ask why you and Miss Lloyd decided to keep it to yourselves?"

I had expected that question. "You should know," I replied, "and at the same time I'm offering my apologies for what must seem a gross discourtesy. You see, the original reason was Veronica's wish. She saw that there was a possible line of defence in that account, but she asked me to say nothing about it because she fears above all things a verdict of guilty but insane and consequent detention in Broadmoor."

To my surprise Hereward laughed grimly. But I checked whatever comment he was about to make.

"One other thing you should know," I continued, "is that I put these facts to Inspector Morris and he insisted that the best course in these circumstances was to keep them quiet. He held the view very strongly that to introduce a defence on those lines after the confession would look too much like over-ingenuity and in the long run do more harm than good."

"I see." Hereward smiled. "If you will forgive me, I think it is a point that you would have done better to discuss with your legal advisers than with the police. But let it pass. I'm not going to throw any bricks about. But I must tell you, Harding, that both you and the Inspector were wrong; yes, utterly wrong."

"Why?"

"Because while Inspector Morris has been putting too much unjustified reliance on prima facie evidence, you, on the other hand, have over-valued the importance of the psychological evidence of personality. Can't you see that?"

"Yes, I see that now and I'm really sorry."

"There's nothing to be sorry about," he said gently. "It's quite obvious to me that your devotion to Miss Lloyd made you promise to keep silent about her sleep-walking."

"Yes. Was I wrong in doing so?"

"Yes. It would have been very wrong if you did keep your promise. But now you have told us all about Miss Lloyd's state of somnambulism, the entire case could be viewed under a different light."

"You don't mean," I asked eagerly "that there might be a chance of acquittal?"

"Not so fast, my friend," he answered. "That I can't promise. It all depends on how the facts of the murder would be presented under these new circumstances. But one thing I can promise you. We – Vanlien and I – would do our damnedest for Miss Lloyd. Have no doubts about that."

"Thank you, thank you with all my heart," was all I could say, trying hard to restrain the tears that were welling in my eyes. "Can I do anything to help?"

"Not at the moment, Harding. Perhaps later we might make use of your knowledge in psychology."

"I would give my own life if that'll help Veronica," I cried in all sincerity.

"I don't think that would help Miss Lloyd," smiled Hereward. "What we've to do – and quickly – is to ask for a postponement of the trial." He rose and turned to Vanlien. "I shall get in touch with the judge at once," he said.

"Do you think the judge will grant a postponement at such a late hour?" asked Vanlien gloomily. I think he felt thoroughly depressed at these last-minute developments.

Hereward nodded. "He'll have to. After presenting the facts he'll have no alternative but to order a postponement in the face of the new evidence," he concluded. His jaws were set very firmly and I had no doubt whatever of the outcome.

"The next thing to do is to get permission from the prison authorities to see Miss Lloyd and thrash things out." Hereward was addressing both of us – Vanlien and me. "I suggest Harding stays here in your office, Vanlien, until I telephone you and then perhaps you'll bring him along with you straight to the prison."

"Do you think you'll get permission for a family party at such a short notice?" smiled Vanlien.

Hereward nodded. "I'll fix it," he said simply.

EIGHT

Time has never passed so slowly for me as it did during my waiting for Hereward's call. Vanlien had taken me to a small, unused office where I waited, looking at my watch every few minutes thinking an hour must have passed.

Hereward obviously intended to do his best and intended to take on a desperate chance and fight to the finish. His attitude certainly made me feel slightly more at ease and I found cause for more courage than I had known for some time. Yet there was little enough to hope for. As my thoughts churned on, I hardly knew whether to be grateful to Hereward or to curse him for raising perhaps hopes where there were none.

When, at last, Vanlien came in, hat in his hand, ready to set out, I sprang to my feet. Automatically I glanced again at my watch. So that eternity had been no more than just over an hour! It seemed incredible to me that Hereward had been able to arrange matters so swiftly. Officialdom moves slowly, yet there it was. Hereward wanted, so Vanlien said, to meet us at Holloway Prison in half an hour. I felt terribly pleased, though what Veronica would say and what she would think of me for betraying her confidence, I barely dared to consider.

Hereward had been able to arrange for the conference to take place in a small, secluded room. It was the first occasion for some time that I had seen Veronica, for I had not been allowed to be present at the meetings between her and the lawyers. My heart leapt as she entered, accompanied by a wardress. She was looking white and drawn, though she seemed in complete command of herself. The faint smile, tinged with sadness, that she gave me would remain for ever as one of my most poignant memories.

Hereward was standing next to me and gave me a quick glance. In his eyes were sympathy and understanding – and warning. He must have guessed my state of hardly controllable excitement.

"Steady," he said softly. "Try to be calm." If I was grateful to him then for those quiet words, I am, looking back on it, still more grateful now. They seemed to cement the friendship that I had felt so suddenly for him earlier in the day.

Veronica looked from one to the other of us with a slightly puzzled air. "I'm pleased to see you all," she said quietly. "May I know to what I owe this unexpected visit?"

I opened my mouth to speak, but again Hereward glanced quickly at me. I remained silent but I couldn't take my eyes from Veronica.

"Miss Lloyd," he began, "we have come here on a very important errand. It seems necessary now to reconsider the whole of our defence. Under pressure from me, Doctor Harding had told me that you believe you killed Samuel Laing in a somnambulistic trance. It's a pity that you did not tell me about it earlier. Now I want your consent to arrange my defence on those lines."

She stared at him in silence and then her eyes turned accusingly and sorrowfully on me. Hereward smiled slightly.

"No – don't blame Dr. Harding," he said quietly and sympathetically. "He's told me everything, including your reason for the suppression of the facts. You've both been misguided and it's better to leave it at that. Now listen to me!"

He told her briefly and succinctly his reasons for bringing the new facts to light. Hereward made his points with a quiet emphasis that was very compelling. The words of repudiation of his suggestion that rose so obviously to Veronica's lips were repressed, and she grew thoughtful.

"I put it to you, Miss Lloyd," he went on, "that we have no alternative but to tell the truth and rely on that to mitigate the crime. In fact, I doubt whether I could consent to any other course. It's the best course from any point of view and I'll be able to arrange for postponement of the trial."

Veronica still remained silent.

I couldn't help feeling that Hereward was right in what he was saying. Yet for all that I could have sunk through the floor when Veronica turned tear-filled eyes upon me.

"Very well, Mr. Hereward," she said in a low voice. "If you think so, I will be guided by you. I'm grateful to Mark – no woman could ask for greater loyalty from a man – but I'm grateful to you, too, for all you have done for me. I'm sorry I've played about with you in this way and caused you so much trouble."

Hereward smiled cordially. "Thank you, Miss Lloyd. In this world, good intentions are all too apt, unfortunately, to go wrong. I have no special regrets because we know now where we stand. And now, as time is running out, I must ask you a few questions."

He became business-like at once, getting details of her somnambulistic adventures and the names and addresses of possible witnesses. Curiously, as he talked, I felt confidence growing in me. The worries and torments that had pursued me all these weeks suddenly died and the old mood of resolution to be defeated by nothing – which, though it may sound conceited, had always been the attitude I have taken to life – returned. The outlook was black in any event. The thought of being parted from Veronica for years still haunted me, but I felt I could now wait for the outcome of the trial in peace, if not in contentment. The hand of friendship – and it was a very strong, supporting hand – had been held out; and in grasping it I had transferred part of my burden to shoulders that were fit and ready to bear it.

Hereward and Vanlien lost no time after that last meeting with Veronica. They arranged to see the judge in charge of her case. In the face of the new evidence they presented, the judge had no alternative but to accede to their request. Two days later a smiling Hereward came to my house in person. He wanted to tell me the good news and to discuss the point of somnambulism in more detail. I was more than grateful for his visit and begged him to stay for dinner.

"Yes, thank you, Harding," he accepted my invitation. "A good dinner and perhaps a glass of wine would do us both good. It's a pity Miss Lloyd cannot be here and share it with us." He smiled at me sympathetically.

"Yes, it is a pity. But we might yet have wine with Veronica," I said with determination.

Hereward looked at me but remained silent for a few moments.

"You know," he changed the subject, "I did have quite a time to convince His Lordship to grant a month's postponement."

"I can imagine only too well," I said quietly.

While we waited for Maggie to call us for dinner I began to feel that something dramatic had happened but also that a new and promising phase had dawned. I felt sure that this emotion sprang from within me, born of the courage and hope that Hereward's personality had somehow infused into me. I believed, though without any logical reason, that the worst was over, and that from now on there would be a steady improvement in the state of things.

Guy Hereward seemed more than pleased at the sight of the succulent steaks Maggie had cooked and the bottle of red Chianti wine.

"Now, Harding, I'm doing the prescribing. Not a word of business till we're through with our food and drink. The two don't mix in my opinion."

It was an enjoyable dinner and when it was over we moved into the small lounge to have our coffee. He lit his pipe and settled himself in one of the two armchairs. I took the other and we faced each other.

"Now we've got to see where we are," he began without further preamble. "Of course, one month is not too much time, but it's enough for me to prepare the new defence."

"There's no chance for an acquittal, I suppose?"

"That, I'm afraid, is quite impossible, but I shall argue for a verdict of unintentional manslaughter."

"I see. So if it could be proved that Veronica was actually sleep-walking at the time – say by producing an eye-witness – there still would be a verdict of manslaughter?"

"I'm afraid so. An acquittal, or even a pardon, could only be achieved if we could produce some new evidence, I mean something that would clearly materially alter the whole atmosphere of the case, and provided entirely fresh questions for judgement."

"I understand. Well, I leave it in your hands."

He smiled. "Thank you, Harding. I'll do my best – you know that."

I nodded. The conversation had started a new train of thought in my mind. The whole ghastly affair could be changed if new evidence of a different kind was forthcoming. My mind was made up. I resolved to reconsider the whole case from that angle. I was certainly not satisfied with the idea of Veronica being sentenced for manslaughter. There was still that thought in the back of my mind that the whole business was a very tragic farce and that something was fundamentally wrong.

It was quite past midnight when Hereward said good night to me and left my house. And I fell asleep almost immediately the moment I went to bed. I slept better that night than I had done for the last few weeks.

As I dressed slowly the next morning, the desire for some activity began to take hold of me. For the first time for several weeks I went to my hospital and my consulting rooms and did my best to bring things there back to normal. I told my receptionist that I could take a limited number of appointments again, but not too many. My secretary, that hard-bitten disillusioned woman, smiled grimly at my apparent ambition to take up work again. I had to enquire as to the cause of her amusement.

The smile broadened. "There'll be two effects on your practice, Doctor," she said in reply. "On the one hand some of your patients will now seek advice elsewhere because they won't wish to associate with a man who's got so much publicity in connection with an impending murder trial – you're in all the papers lately, you know, with the story of your fiancée being arrested and possibly being indicted with murder. A very nice story for the Fleet Street boys."

She looked at me rather mockingly, and I blushed – yes, actually blushed – with indignation and confusion. I had not thought of this particular aspect of the affair.

"On the other hand," she continued, "you'll get quite a rush of would-be patients during the next few days before the trial – people who would be quite ready to pay your fees merely for the pleasure of being able to say to their friends that they've been to see the notorious Dr. Harding whose fiancée is indicted for murder! May I offer a word of advice?"

"Well?" I asked, without trying to hide my annoyance in her interference with my affairs.

"Just this, Doctor. Start work again if you feel like it – it will probably do you good. But leave it to me to accept appointments only when the people come to you with a letter of introduction from one of your doctor-friends. That'll keep the sensation-mongers out of it."

Suddenly she grew intently serious.

"Please don't think me impertinent, Doctor," she said, "but I really feel for you. I imagine you must be going through hell, and I only hope there is some way out of it – for yours and Miss Lloyd's sake."

"Thanks," I said briefly but sincerely. "And about your advice, it's good as usual and I leave it to you to go ahead."

"Right-ho!" she said, not very respectfully. "What are your plans for today?"

"I'll be making my usual rounds at the hospital and then I shall be at home, so far as I know."

"I see. I shall know where to get you then. If you're out and there are any appointments for tomorrow I'll leave a message."

We settled down to clearing some of the arrears of correspondence. There was not a great deal of it, for she had worked wonders in keeping routine affairs going.

When I returned late that afternoon to my house, still wrapped up in my new speculations about Veronica's case, I felt quite annoyed when I found a message waiting for me. It was about an old patient, an elderly gentleman named Mathers, whom I had treated at intervals over a period of years. He was in town, the message said, and wished to know if I could see him that afternoon. He would be calling again about five o'clock on the off chance that I might be in. Rather annoyed, I was on the point of telephoning that I should be unable to see him when I checked myself. Why not? There was nothing much wrong with old Mathers and if I was to get into harness again, a start had to be made some time.

I returned to my rooms almost exactly at five o'clock and found Mathers waiting for me. He had that curiously fresh pink complexion which some elderly men have and the wisps of white hair which stuck out round his bald pate like a halo gave him a very cherubic appearance. He might have served a comic paper artist as a model for the perfect uncle.

"How do, Harding?" he said when he was shown in. "I thought I'd just look you up as I was in town again for the day. Don't come up much nowadays, you know."

"I'm always glad to see you," I replied. "Anything special the matter?"

He shook his head. "A few nightmares lately – but I expect that's the food we eat nowadays, if you psychologists will admit so commonplace an explanation."

"Certainly," I said. "Bad digestion naturally leads to bad dreams. God knows why it should."

"Don't ask me," he chuckled. "That's what people pay you fees for, so it would be indiscreet for me to make a suggestion." He chatted on for a while and then suddenly he turned a grave eye on me.

"I wonder if I may refer to a delicate subject," he began cautiously. "Of course, I've read about yours and your fiancée's trouble, and I hardly can say how sorry I am. I can understand what you're going through." He smiled at me warmly.

"Thank you, Mathers," I said. "It's nice of you to feel like that."

"Yes, Harding, I'm really sorry for Miss Lloyd. But the case interested me from another point of view – apart from my personal interest in you, you know. You see it took me back to my youth" – he sighed a little melodramatically –

"to the days before Conan Doyle set the fashion for detective stories and we read Wilkie Collins. Remember 'The Moonstone'?"

I nodded. What the blazes would that book, a classic of its kind, have to do with it? And why in the name of common decency had he got to bring it up now, when it was the last subject on earth I wanted to discuss – especially with a comparative stranger. But Mathers was a garrulous old man and talked for the sake of talking. So I bore with him as patiently as I could.

"Then you'll recall how that book worked out. In the end, you remember, it was established that the jewel was stolen by a man walking in his sleep, after he'd suffered some kind of shock – I believe by cutting off smoking suddenly. Maybe you psychologists just laugh at it, but it's a good yarn and a great favourite of mine."

"I can't remember it clearly to analyse it professionally," I replied. "But I suppose you'll find a parallel for almost everything in fiction in real life."

He nodded. "And the old adage about truth being stranger than fiction still holds," he added.

After that I got rid of him as soon as I decently could. I was tired to death with his chatter. Mathers left with promises to call again when next he was in town, but I did not encourage him; I just uttered a few conventional words of politeness. Was this what it was going to be like from now on? Would it be impossible for me to escape the talk and gossip of that case, even from my old patients? And what would happen, when or if Veronica was sentenced? I felt inclined then and there to give up practice altogether until the case was settled one way or the other. But I told myself not to be foolish. The time for drastic decisions on my future lay ahead still – though not, perhaps, so very far ahead.

NINE

It was in the evening when I was enjoying a quiet pipe after a dinner at home that my thoughts returned to old Mathers and his chatter. I was in some way interested in what he had said despite my resentment at the time. I even went so far as to take a copy of 'The Moonstone' down from my shelves where it had lain untouched for years, and skim through the story, which is one of the masterpieces of characterization in detective fiction and in its way a work of art.

I sat down again and settled myself to think. There is an odd feeling which most of us experience at some time – a feeling that a thought or an idea is on its way, knocking at the door, so to speak, until we find the key that will enable us to open the entrance to it. It is, of course, just an expression of some content of the unconscious welling up and trying to break through into consciousness. But a re-statement in psycho-analytical terms does not alter in any way the validity and vividness of the experience.

For quite a long time I sat with no particular thought in mind – only that feeling that something was about to come to me. And then I realised that the waiting thought was one of accusation. I had done nothing. I had never studied the problem of Veronica's affairs from my own professional standpoint. I was shocked and annoyed with myself. All this time I had been going about with the idea that the whole thing was a terrible mistake, but I had never sat down and considered it objectively – particularly as the case itself involved questions that lay very clearly within the field of my speciality.

This was a new and exciting thought. I must think it out. I had accepted Veronica's explanation and Inspector Morris's carefully marshalled facts. No doubt they were right, but I had no proof that they were. I did not doubt either Veronica or Dick, but it might be there was something else that neither of them had seen – something that had evaded even Hereward's clear brain, though of that possibility I was more than a little sceptical.

The more I considered it, the more foolish I began to think myself. I had taken too much for granted while protesting that Dick and the police did not see far enough. The facts of the murder I had accepted as beyond all doubt. But were they? For the first time, it seemed to me that I had let almost everything be taken by default.

What was the truth as I believed it? Simply that driven to desperation, Veronica had played with the idea of killing Samuel Laing, that she had bought the dagger and then, in a somnambulistic trance, had actually committed the murder. It was a simple and conclusive story. And as I thought that, the comment passed through my mind: "Too simple and too conclusive".

There were psychological factors involved here into which I felt I ought to delve more deeply. I was letting my thoughts run on without ordered control and letting all angles present themselves to me. Suddenly I thought of Guy's words that morning: that the trial could take quite a new aspect if there were really outstanding new evidence. Suppose the new evidence lay just there – in those fields where I was qualified to harvest? It was an exciting and heartening thought. It was hardly believable, but the desire for action was strong in me; it had been ever since our last interview with Veronica. I had glanced at one of the more sensational papers, but I had read no more than the headlines: "Harley Street doctor's fiancée indicted for murder." It had filled me with nausea – actual physical nausea.

Was that story really consistent psychologically? Now I was getting down to work. My restlessness left me. I had the impression that something might come of this. I rose from my chair and began to walk up and down in the room.

I barely noticed when my housekeeper entered to say she was going to bed if there was nothing more needed. She was used to my midnight cogitations anyway and she would not notice if I gave no reply.

That night I barely closed my eyes. I argued with myself and could see no flaw. Veronica had got into a very confused mental state. That was shown in many ways, but in none more clearly than that she had feared to tell me the truth. She had seen a danger to me and had thought that the only way to guard against it was by her own sacrifice and her own effort. It was a reversal of all our shared ideas – that we could trust each other in all things.

In that mood, then, her mind had taken to desperate thoughts: a setting aside of the rational, and a reaching out for the impossible which would put all things right in a trice. It is, of course, an expression of regression to an infantile level.

Veronica's thoughts had turned to murder – to the elimination of the danger that threatened both her and me. Her clear mind had told her that the man was worthless, but the special conditions in it set aside the ordered course of behaviour. In her mind she thought she was above the limitations that applied to ordinary human beings.

At this stage, it is doubtful if any actual intention of murder existed in her conscious mind. Playing with the idea was a fantasy satisfaction, a relief for the mind from the tortures of her problems. Though such fantasy reliefs are the signposts on the road to neurosis, they have their uses. A person can sometime work out the most horrible thoughts by finding some similar kind of mental satisfaction. This, I thought, is what happened when Veronica bought the dagger – to protect herself against Samuel Laing. Her thoughts would be almost entirely in the sense of passive protection rather than of active aggression, consciously, at any rate. She was staving off danger. One does not run out of the house to meet a storm but prepares, by closing the windows, for the worst.

There, in all probability the matter would have ended. The mere purchase of the weapon would have satisfied the unconscious wish in her. For the whole thing was, in the light of what I knew of her personality, very significant. I knew her horror of weapons of all kinds. The mere sight of some ancient firearms and swords in a museum we had visited together once, had quite upset her. Yet here she was buying a dagger and taking it home to her flat. It was all of a piece with a wish-fulfilment.

In her sleep, these unconscious stirrings would gain almost complete control of her personality, for it is in sleep that our tensions are largely relieved through dreams. But Veronica was subject to somnambulism, which is held by some authorities to be a special form of dream realisation. It provides a more active outlet for the contained, unconscious pressure. The subject is able to work out in motor action ideas that cannot wholly be satisfied by dream images.

This, I felt, was Veronica's state. The murder wish gained possession of her and it had brought her to a condition in which it demanded release. Her tendency towards somnambulism had been her undoing. If she had been normal she might have worked it out in dreams. She had committed the murder, but it had not actually been her true self. The thing which had killed was her unconscious.

I sat down again, feeling a little exhausted by my intense thoughts. Yes, the picture was consistent and plausible enough. All I had done was to restate, in more elaborate terms, what we already knew. With my eyes closed I sat back and went all over it again. I could find no flaw. All my hopes of finding something new and arresting were dashed to the ground. Believing I had acquitted Veronica in my own mind, I had only succeeded in convincing myself of her actual guilt.

It must have been a considerable time that I sat there. I must have dozed for a short while when I awoke with a start. It was just as if someone had come in and plucked my by the sleeve to rouse me. I very nearly sprang to my feet, but then I realised that there was no physical intruder. It was my thoughts calling me to active consciousness with a blinding light that almost shocked my brain.

The chiming clock in the hall struck two. At that hour of morning I saw the fallacy. From that moment my whole outlook changed. I believed I could not only bring about a verdict of manslaughter, but gain an acquittal for Veronica whose life was more to me than my own.

For the rest of the night, until the grey light of dawn crept across the sky, I was busy turning up in my mind the authorities, setting this view against that and balancing them by my own experience and knowledge. It was a hard task, but when at last I sank exhausted and fully dressed upon my bed, I believed that something could be done, even though the theory of it had still yet to be fully worked out. And just before I fell asleep, worn out by my mental exertions, a single thought came to me with such vividness that I remember the shock of it after all this time. It was that, when the light of day and reason came, my theory might prove to be little more than moonshine.

TEN

By midday, after a long and sound sleep, I had been able to review the results of my night's labours. The doubt I had experienced on falling asleep did not persist. I was now confident enough to telephone Guy Hereward and ask if I could see him as soon as convenient. Without asking any questions, he said we could meet at his chambers after lunch. I was pleased to notice that he sounded quite eager, although I gave him no indication of my reasons for asking for an appointment.

As soon as I was shown into his room, he looked at me with a questioning air. "Well?" he said. "What brings you here, Harding? I assume it must be something to do with our case. Am I right?"

"Yes, you're right."

"Something new?" he asked.

I nodded. "I've been doing some hard thinking," I began, "and I've come to the conclusion that all of us have been led astray by too obvious appearances in this case. I think we've been wrong all along the line in the whole argument."

"Ah!" He made no sign of being sceptical. On the contrary, he almost appeared to expect my statement.

"Yes," he went on, "that's why I've been so interested in this case. It's been too easy for the prosecution. Everything seems to be playing into their hands. I've searched for a fallacy myself and spent a good many hours in the hunt, but so far it's eluded me. So you think it lies up your street?"

"Reviewing the whole affair from my own angle," I answered, "at first it looked all right – in fact, I almost convinced myself I was bashing my head against a brick wall. But then light dawned, and – well, I'd better tell you about it."

In some detail I told him of my original review and my conclusion that the whole thing was sound. He nodded.

"It sounds quite convincing to me. Where's the weak point?"

I laughed and that seemed to surprise him.

"I'll tell you another curious thing," I replied, and gave him a brief account of Mather's gossip. "Perhaps his talk of 'The Moonstone' may have started my thoughts off on somnambulism," I went on, "but that's not the vital point. He told me also he'd been having bad dreams and said they were probably due to indigestion. It was the memory of Mather's gossip that flashed across my mind and set me off on a new track which I think is the right one."

"I don't think I quite understand," Hereward commented slowly.

"No. Just as I couldn't follow some of your legal arguments, I expect." I drew a deep breath. I knew that this was to be the greatest possible test.

"Well, this is the point," I went on. "That stupid bit of talk came back to me – I was half dozing at the time – and the reply I might have made rose to my mind. The dream content is determined by the unconscious and they are largely determined by childhood experiences which have been repressed. That is why nightmares tend to run to pattern and repeat themselves so often. The fears of childhood are revived in an acutely distressing symbolic form."

"That's quite interesting," he observed, "but how does it bear on our case and Veronica's somnambulism?"

"Because it drew my attention to the basic principle. The stuff that comes out in dreams is the deep-seated material, very rarely the superficial one. It's true that the symbolism may be influenced by experiences during the day, but that's only a fresh cloak for the older ones. Practically all dream experience springs from the deep unconscious and not from the freshly repressed material."

"You're getting rather technical and involved," Guy commented, "but I think I grasp your point, even though I can't see its bearing yet. You mean that a person only dreams, in the majority of cases, of events far back in his life?"

"Roughly – yes." I proceeded: "It fits into the case like this. Let us accept for the moment that somnambulism is an active form of dream experience. The subject does not merely see his symbolic fantasies with the inner eye, as a picture in the mind, but actually lives through some of them by motor activity of which he is unconscious. Somnambulists don't often do rational things, you know. Some sleep-walkers climb roofs they wouldn't attempt in waking moments and so on. Somnambulistic activity is, in the main, as irrational and symbolic as dreaming; in fact you might almost call it a mimed dream."

"I think I'm beginning to see where all this is leading," Guy remarked with some enthusiasm.

"You see," I resumed, "the point is this: according to the ideas we've had up to now, Veronica committed the murder while she was in a somnambulistic trance, as a relief for her pent-up murder wishes. But those wishes were of very recent repression; in fact, they were hardly repressed at all because she was able to recognize them at once and actually bought the dagger under their influence. Now if the likelihood of dream experience being recent is small, it follows that the likelihood of somnambulistic activity being a release for recent repressions is even smaller. The main safety valve doesn't blow till the heater is working at its utmost."

"Yes," he put in eagerly. "What next?"

"Now no one could allege that murder wishes were a normal part of Veronica's personality," I continued. "If she sleep-walked that night she was doing so to work out something deeper. The troubles of the moment might have led her to the somnambulistic state, but they would hardly be enacted in it. Therefore, the chances that she did the murder in her sleep are very small."

Guy Hereward sat back and half closed his eyes. "That's an interesting point and I think you've made out a case," he said, "but it doesn't altogether lead to practical action. No Court would accept that theory in contradiction of the proved facts, like the fingerprints and so on."

"There I agree with you. But it's a starting point. As it stands, the theory itself is not watertight, for there is the remote chance that a very vivid recent experience might be re-lived in a dream or in somnambulism."

He chuckled. "You psychologists get a somewhat jaundiced view of human behaviour," he said, "but I'm not saying you aren't right. All the same, it doesn't suggest any immediate action to me."

"No. But it is strengthened by another viewpoint. There are very close similarities between somnambulism and the behaviour of people under hypnosis. According to some authorities, in somnambulism the mind responds to the unconscious as in hypnotism it does to the suggestion of the hypnotist."

"Well? That doesn't look promising to me. It might mean that Veronica, having repressed her murder wish in waking hours, acted under unconscious auto-suggestion while asleep."

"That's true. But there's one point here that is important. In the earlier days of hypnotism it was believed that if the suggestion was powerful enough, the subject could be made to do anything, no matter what it might be. A victim of a hypnotist could commit murders for him, though leading normally a blameless life."

"Isn't that so, then?"

"As a rule, no. You can't induce a hypnotized subject to do things which are alien to the personality. Therapy by suggestion is a sort of one-way street. The patient wants to get better or overcome some bad habit and you can suggest that the desired result will come about. Either it does come about or there is no improvement, but hypnotic suggestion won't make things worse. All it does is to remove barriers in the way of progress and so enable the patient's desire for better health to work itself out. That's the one-way street. You can either go forward or stop, but you can't go backwards."

"I see. This is very interesting." Guy spoke slowly.

"I think you see my point, Guy," I smiled. "If Veronica was acting under the suggestion of her unconscious in a hypnotic way, she would be most unlikely to commit murder. The very thought of killing anything is repugnant to her. That is a deep-seated characteristic of hers. So, even if we assume that the unconscious suggested to her in her somnambulistic state that the murder could be committed then and there, the deep layers of her personality would protect her. The act would be against her ingrained desires. The superficial and transient couldn't take charge of the enduring and deep-seated."

"So from two points of view and on two different conceptions of somnambulism, there is a very strong suggestion that the whole idea of murder during her sleep-walking is almost impossible." He paused for reflection and I did not interrupt him. At last he spoke again slowly.

"I think you've got on to something very important here, Mark, though what we are to make of it I don't quite know. It may convince you and it may convince me, but I can hardly see that it would sound well in Court, even if we got as far. I cannot see, for the life of me, how we can convince both judge and jury that Veronica is incapable of committing murder."

He paused again.

"Have you any suggestions?" he asked, giving me a keen glance.

I had. And I told him what they were.

When I had finished talking, Guy looked at me with a serious expression.

"It's a difficult job at any event," he said, "and especially in a murder case trial. Let's tackle the simplest part first. I'd better see the people at Scotland Yard and see what I can do about that side of it."

"No need for that," I said, shaking my head. "I'll see Inspector Morris – he's a great friend of mine as you know – and he'll do everything that can be done. He hates this case, though it is a gift to him, but no one would be better pleased than he, if we can get an acquittal."

"Very well, then. And I think the second part must rest on the results of the first. I mean, if your results are positive then I have better grounds for approaching the judge. But I shan't remain idle while you're busy with the Yard. I'll put out a few feelers and see some people I know who're in a position to help. We've almost a whole month before the trial and we mustn't rely on breaking down the front door. If I can find a back window open, I won't hesitate to jump in."

I grinned and asked if I might use the telephone. He pushed the instrument towards me. And when I dialled the notorious number he smiled. Inspector Morris was available and I spoke to him at once. Yes, he would see me – as soon as I liked. But he seemed puzzled when I said it was urgent and about Veronica. I told him I would explain at our interview.

"Well, Mark, what is it now that's so urgent?" he asked the moment we shook hands. "I hope you're not stirring up more muddy waters."

"What we're going to do," I replied, "is to produce new evidence and get Veronica acquitted. We've all of us been led astray by taking the obvious facts for granted."

He grimaced. "I'm sorry, Mark, if I don't seem enthusiastic. The whole thing has been a real nightmare to me and I'm amazed that you can still have hopes of an acquittal."

I looked at him rather curiously. This was quite unlike Dick. "I know how much trouble this case has been to you, and I'm very grateful for all the help you have given to me and to Veronica. You have been a good friend, but I shouldn't bother you now without good cause – you know that. I've discussed this new turn of events with Hereward and it's on his suggestion that I've come along here. I say that to show you that it isn't just a bee in my bonnet – you know Guy Hereward well enough to realise he wouldn't back any absurdity. I've got a great favour to ask you, Dick, but I want you to see right from the start that it isn't just to satisfy a whim."

He gave me a keen look. "I'm sorry, Mark," he said genuinely, "I didn't mean to be so unpleasant. If you've really got something important to discuss, then I'm your man. You know I would do anything in my power to help Veronica. What is it you want, Mark?"

"I want to go back to the beginning and do some of the things we should have done then – or at least I should. I know, Dick, you don't like psychological theories. Neither do judges or juries, but our position is that a psychological review of the case has given certain new suggestions that are worth following up and if we can get any help from you in Scotland Yard we shall try for an acquittal."

"That sounds pretty sweeping, but I can't imagine Hereward giving his O.K. unless he was very well satisfied – it takes a lot to convince him. Tell me all about this new turn of events and then we'll see together what can be done."

I told him briefly and succinctly about my theory. He listened with great attention and nodded from time to time.

"Of course, it's just theory – and far-fetched theory at that. What does Guy Hereward think?"

"He thinks it is definitely worth following up," I replied, "and he's taking certain preliminary action on his own side which we needn't go into now, because whether it comes into the open or not depends upon the results of my visit here. I don't want to trespass on your kindness, Dick, but I want to examine, if I can, the photographs of the crime, the medical report and see the dagger again. Can that be arranged?"

"Why?" he demanded. "They've all been examined by experts, and I don't think anybody else could possibly get anything more out of them."

"No. Perhaps not. But my point is that all of us have taken too much for granted. Those things have been examined with a certain hypothesis in mind, a hypothesis that was accepted as true right from the outset. I want to look at them again with another theory in mind."

"It'll be difficult," he said reflectively. "I can't simply get hold of the dossier and hand it over to you, can I now?" He thought for a moment. "I think the best way would be for Hereward to get in touch with the A.C. – no, with the Commissioner – and tell him confidentially that certain new information has come to hand and it is vital that you, as an expert, should be allowed to make the examination you want."

"Right, Dick. I'll go and see Hereward at once and ask for his help the way you suggest."

Dick rose and held his hand. "Off the record, Mark," he smiled at me, "if you get a refusal – and God knows how the official mind works – you, my friend, shall have that dossier though it might cost me my job. I can't swallow the whole of your theory, but I must confess that it's given me one of the best moments I've known for a long time. It gives me a thrill to think that there might be just a little ray of hope in this ghastly business."

"How can I thank you, Dick, for all that you're doing for Veronica and me?"

"Don't thank me, Mark. I only hope that your theory will work." His mouth shut firmly and I knew that he wanted no further comments on his action. Dick is like that. So I did not say a word more. I just pressed his hand warmly and left.

I had made a small step forward, though I could have wished I had done more.

ELEVEN

Guy did not look very pleased when I told him the result of my interview.

"I'd hoped you'd get hold of the stuff right away, but I suppose Morris is right," he said. "I'll get in touch with the Commissioner right away. Luckily I've met him several times, so I can make it a more or less friendly contact."

"I did my best to get hold of the dossier, but Morris was adamant," I informed him.

"Oh, I know Inspector Morris is a stickler where the law is concerned." Guy smiled. "I'll get on to the Commissioner at once."

He made his telephone call and the way he handled it delighted me. He refused politely but firmly to be put off by underlings of any kind and so at last spoke to Sir George Poole himself. The result was satisfactory. Guy insisted that the case was very urgent and the Commissioner agreed to see him that very day.

"You can take me there in your car," said Guy, "and you're coming to the interview with me. It may be very useful to have my expert witness and coadjutor on the spot."

Pleased with this arrangement, I led the way to the car park and in a very short time we were in Scotland Yard. After only a brief wait we were both shown into the Commissioner's office.

As Guy introduced me, I took a quick survey of Sir George Poole. He was the first civilian Commissioner the Metropolitan Police had had for a considerable time, but for all that he might, from his appearance, well have been thought to be a retired officer. His face was lined and keen and his hair was greying. He held his tall, spare body very upright and there was a precision about every move of his – more common in military men than in civilians. He had been a barrister before he had come to Scotland Yard, though his appearances in Court had been few.

There was warmth in his greeting, but he was by no means effusive. Obviously he was used to plunging straight into business without conveying any sense of discourtesy or haste.

It was Guy who explained what we wanted. He did so courteously but also with a sense of urgency and it was clear that Sir George was impressed. After he had listened to Guy he glanced at me.

"I am going to ask you, Doctor, for an outline of your theory," he said. "This is neither curiosity, nor any desire on my part to find out what your thoughts are so that we of the police can counteract them." Sir George paused for a moment, clearing his throat. "I'm interested in the application of modern psychology to crime," he went on, "though in official circles even a commissioner has to keep that in the background. I can assure you, however, that anything you tell me, I shall regard as a personal favour and a disclosure in complete confidence. It will also enable me to judge whether I am justified in granting what you ask."

"Certainly, Sir George," said Guy quickly. "We appreciate your interest and Dr. Harding will be only too pleased to tell you all about it."

So, for the third time, I gave a resumé of my line of thought. The reaction from Sir George was a slight smile, the exact nature of which I could not discover at that time.

"Very ingenious, Doctor," he commented, "though as Hereward has probably told you, it would make a poor show in Court. But I think it's sufficient ground for reopening the investigation. Gentlemen, it has been my ambition and policy to make sure that C.I.D. fully discharges its function of investigating crime impartially to get at the truth, with no desire of securing a conviction at any price. I said just now that what you have put before me justifies the new line of investigation. I propose to issue instructions that Inspector Morris shall go into it all again in close collaboration with you two, in order to discover if something has been overlooked and fresh evidence can be obtained. Is that course acceptable to you?"

I did not feel enthusiastic myself, for I did not see that any useful purpose would be served by it; but Guy welcomed the suggestion warmly.

"Our thanks are due to you, Sir George," he replied graciously. "We believed you would give us help, but hardly expected the collaboration you propose."

Sir George smiled again under this courteous broadside and spoke into his desk telephone. In a few minutes Inspector Morris came into the room.

"Oh, Morris," said Sir George, "I think you know these gentlemen and it's even possible you know why they are here." Again that quiet smile crossed his lips. "I have listened to a statement from them and I think that the Lloyd case had better be reinvestigated. I want it to be a thorough investigation almost as though it were an entirely fresh case. You can use all the normal services and personnel as necessary. The only stipulation is that you must keep these two gentlemen informed fully and all the time."

"Yes, sir," said Dick. "I'll see that your instructions are carried out."

"I suggest that no time is lost. If these two gentlemen have the time now, perhaps they could go with you and discuss the preliminaries. You agree, Hereward, that there is no time to lose," he added, looking at Guy.

Guy nodded. "I do, Sir George," he replied. "We've less than a month to carry out this new line of approach."

"You should know better than anyone else how difficult and time consuming such investigations can be."

Guy smiled and rose. Sir George shook hands and in a few minutes we were in Inspector Morris's small office.

"You people seem to know how to get what you want," he said, leaning back in his chair. "I didn't expect the Old Man to go quite so far as he has done, but there it is. As a matter of fact, I'm not sure whether by dragging me in again he has paid me a compliment or an insult."

Inspector Morris spoke without bitterness or malice, but I knew him well enough to understand that he was more than willing to take on the task of seeing if things could be put right or improved on. A lesser man would have felt slighted and perhaps become antagonistic. Not so Dick. His passion was for truth – and truth no matter what the cost.

"I've orders not to waste time," he smiled grimly. "The sooner I get this thing out of my system the better for everyone. I'll get on to C.R.O. and have everything brought up."

He picked up the telephone and gave his instructions. There was apparently some demurring at the other end of the line, for he suddenly said, very tersely: "Commissioner's orders. If you don't like it, refer it to him."

We settled down to wait in silence. It was only a few minutes later, however, when a messenger arrived with a box and a large file, which he placed on the desk. Dick signed to us to draw our chairs nearer.

"This is the lot," he said. "The box contains the knife and

the file has all the papers, photographs and sketches. What shall we look at first?" He glanced at Guy, but he nodded to me.

"I think it's Mark's show," he remarked. "You and I, Dick, play the part of the sceptical audience."

I opened the box with trembling hand. So this was the weapon! It was a thin-bladed knife with a bronze shaft and the scabbard which lay alongside it in the box was of some parchment material or bark, inlaid with brasswork. On the haft were the developed and set fingerprints. They were Veronica's fingerprints, there was no doubt about that. On the blade were some stains, now oxidized with age but obviously bloodstains. My thoughts began to wander – with Veronica in her cell, reviving memories of hopes that were now dead, of happy days and hours that would never return. For whatever happened now, if Veronica were to come into that room on that very instant, a free woman, life could never be quite the same again. Perhaps the sight of the dagger brought this realisation for me, surprisingly for the very first time. Until now I had clung stubbornly to our life, to our plans as they were before. Now I knew at last that all was changed, all was gone. A storm may bring new life to a garden and give it revived beauty, but it is a new beauty and that which it was before has forever departed. So it was with us. There were new and uncharted seas to traverse – perhaps alone, perhaps together. Who knew the answer? I was suddenly aware of two pairs of eyes fixed upon me and I realised how much good this awful experience had brought to me in deepening the friendship of one man and leading me to the friendship of another. My mood of introspection passed and I forced a smile to my lips.

"I'm sorry," I said softly. "The sight of this knife rather upset me."

"If you want to start with the dagger," said Dick gruffly –

I think my show of emotion had rather moved his normally tranquil spirit – "the best thing to do is to study the photographs that were taken at the time. Here they are."

He drew out a large envelope from the dossier and handed it to me. Slowly I drew out the batch of wholeplate prints it contained.

I looked at the first print showing the dagger as it had lain on the floor in Laing's room. Then another one showing an enlargement of the haft with the fingerprints. The other photographs were enlargements of the bloodstains, showing more clearly their distribution and their shape. It was a complete record of the dagger in its role of the murder weapon.

It is a very curious and striking emotion when a recent experience repeats itself almost exactly but in different circumstances. As I handed back the prints to Dick, I felt such an emotion. Once again I felt as though I was being jerked from a comatose state into a condition of vivid awareness by some external agency. And as before, in the small hours of the morning, I knew that I had seen a fresh facet of the truth.

I looked at Dick. On his face sat an expression that was half puzzlement and half astonishment. So he had seen it too! But I did not speak then about my thoughts.

"Have you the medical report?" I asked, trying to keep my voice as steady as possible.

Without a word, though he gave me a penetrating and encouraging glance, Dick produced the typewritten sheets from the file. I glanced through them quickly, paying particular attention to the paragraph headed 'Nature and Extent of Wounds and Injuries'. When I laid it down, I knew that my thoughts had received confirmation. Still I made no comment. I simply passed the report back to Dick, open at the sheet containing the paragraph I had just mentioned.

He nodded as though he fully understood my purpose. Then I sat back in my chair and looked at Guy, who had taken no part in the proceedings so far.

He was eying us intently and a little smile hovered round his lips.

We all three of us sat in silence for a few moments. Then it was Guy who spoke first.

"Well?" he asked. "You two have been glaring at those papers and photographs without saying a thing. Won't you let me in on your secrets?"

"No, Guy," Dick roused himself. "There are no secrets, but I am inclined to believe that Mark was right when he told me we'd all of us been misled by the obvious."

"Suppose you tell us the reason for all this self-accusation?" Guy suggested.

Dick shook his head. "No. This is Mark's day out. He started this interview and I'm pretty certain he's seen what I've seen. So I'll leave it to him."

"Thank you, Dick," I said slowly. Then I looked straight at Guy. "All this factual evidence we couldn't get round," I went on, "the crux of the whole affair – well, it is quite conclusive. But what it proves is that whoever did the murder, it wasn't Veronica."

"Isn't that rather a sweeping statement?" Guy asked incredulously.

"No, it isn't, Guy," said Dick quietly. "I don't know how I or the others missed it, but it's plain as a pikestaff. But let Mark explain the things he's seen."

"Yes, there's no doubt about it," I said slowly. "Let's start with the bloodstains on the dagger. We'd assumed from Veronica's confession that the dagger was used to kill Laing. In that case the dagger would have been very bloody – all of it. And because the weapon penetrated the arch of the aorta there would be very violent spurting of blood. Those spurts would leave characteristic marks – broad at one end and tapering to a point at the other – with the broad end away from the origin of the blood." I paused for a brief moment.

"Go on, Mark!" Guy pressed eagerly.

"Well, there's not a stain of that kind on the knife," I went on. "The bloodstains are more or less circular with little spreading. This means that they are the result of blood dripping on to the blade while it was lying flat on the floor. That knife, if bloodstains mean anything, has never been in a wound at all!"

Dick nodded. "Yes. The appearance is so obvious and typical that it's incredible how we missed it."

"This is breathtaking," commented Guy. "Anything else, Mark?"

"Yes, the fingerprints. The impressions are quite clear, particularly the one of the index finger. Oh, yes, they're Veronica's all right. But they happen to be all in the wrong places."

"The wrong places?" Guy picked up the photograph I passed to him and nodded slowly. He did not need to be told the rest.

"It's obvious, isn't it?" I continued. "That knife was held point upwards. It would have been extremely difficult for anyone to stab with the hand in that position, don't you think? Almost impossible in fact. And there's no blurring of the prints anywhere. If that dagger had been used for any considerable blow, there would certainly have been some blurring of the prints. It all points out that the knife was carried perhaps point upwards and then suddenly dropped by an opening of the hand."

"I see," Guy nodded again thoughtfully.

"More than that. The fatal wound must be very deep in order to reach the arch of the aorta. In fact it's so deep that it's extremely difficult to believe that a girl like Veronica would have sufficient strength to make it. Put that aside and give her the strength required. Then she'd have to grasp that dagger haft very strongly in her clenched hand. But there are prints of the tips of the fingers only and on opposite sides – I mean, fingers on one side of the haft, thumb on the other, as though it was just lightly held. The picture does not match up anywhere."

"You've put it all quite clearly, Mark," acknowledged Dick. "I'm still kicking myself for overlooking it all and as for the experts – well ... Still the main fault lies with me. I gave them the dagger and said, in effect, 'Are these Veronica's dabs or not?' They gave me the right answer."

"Didn't the surgeon say anything about the wound needing more strength than a woman's?" asked Guy.

I turned the pages of the medical report and read: ' "The wound is of great depth and must have been inflicted by someone possessed of considerable strength. The avoidance of all bony structures is also remarkable. This means that the murderer has had either a fairly accurate anatomical knowledge or it was all the work of chance, which is highly improbable."

"No, that doesn't rule out Veronica as such. A woman could, I suppose, exercise the strength." Guy creased his brow. "But not so likely in the circumstances. She might if she was defending herself from attack."

"I agree with you, there," said Dick. "As it stands, it seems to me that the actual conditions rule out Veronica and almost any other woman. They suggest, in fact, a pretty hefty man not necessarily with anatomical knowledge, as the report hints, but certainly with a knowledge of knifing." Dick paused and turned to Guy. "Don't you think I'm right in my assumption?"

"Yes, Dick. As a matter of fact I think that we have almost too much to go on with." Guy relaxed into his chair a little and prepared himself to talk. "We've moved very fast and far from our point of origin," he went on. "We came here to look for further evidence if it could be found. What we've done is to discover that practically the whole of our facts were wrong in the first place because everything seemed so obvious. Let's have a look round to find where we've arrived at. May we smoke in here?" he asked, looking at Dick who nodded and produced his own pipe and pouch.

"Now," said Guy, when he had got his pipe well alight, "we've got to face up to some pretty startling facts. Samuel Laing was murdered – that cannot be disputed. He was killed by knifing and we can't get away from the fact that Veronica was in the room, either at, or very close to, the actual time of death. Those footprints prove that, so does the dagger. So we have the case of murder by some person unknown with Veronica present in very compromising circumstances. It's no wonder she confessed so readily. If she was there in a somnambulistic trance, she wouldn't know anything about it. But it's difficult to see exactly what happened. Any suggestions?"

Guy looked from Dick to me and back again, but for the moment neither of us spoke. It was Dick who spoke first.

"There are all sorts of other incongruities," he remarked. "How did the blood get on the knife? Why was it there? Why was Veronica there, for that matter? I think we can take it for granted that Veronica was there either just before or immediately after the murder – even while it was being perpetrated. So we have the rather galling position of having the rarest of all things – a murder with an eye-witness who to all intents and purposes was too blind to see."

I chuckled in spite of myself.

"Personally, I think we need an interval for reflection on the next move," Guy concluded. "Will you come back with me, Mark?"

"Yes. I think it's a good idea," I answered. "What about you, Dick?"

Dick stretched himself. "It's O.K. with me."

"It's a very curious position," he remarked as we three rose from our chairs.

"What's that?" asked Guy.

"The Old Man was right when he said the case had to be re-investigated. On a stale trail I've got to find out who it was that knifed dear little Samuel Laing. In any case, Mark, you've got a lot to look forward to now, haven't you? Veronica is safe. You can leave her side of it in Guy's hands and I've to find the murderer. Quite a prospect, isn't it?" He smiled grimly.

"One thing I'll do," said Guy with determination. "I shall have to pull a few strings and hope to ease Veronica's position. We cannot have bail in murder cases, but I will see that she's made as comfortable as possible, poor girl."

I smiled gratefully at Guy while we both shook hands with Dick Morris. We left him to deal with the problems these new developments had caused in the routine life of Scotland Yard.

TWELVE

Guy was very thoughtful when we were alone in his flat in St. John's Wood. He did not speak for some time and silently pointed to the bottle of sherry. We both poured ourselves a glass and drank the liquid slowly.

How wonderful it was to think that Veronica would soon be free. We had managed, at the very first stroke, to cut the shackles that held her. She was not, as we had thought, the unhappy victim of a curious distortion of the mind – for that is what somnambulism is – but actually guiltless of the crime. And how I cursed myself that although I always believed in her innocence, I had not, till this late hour, done anything practical about it, and, as a result, she had been detained in prison for all these terrible weeks.

It was no use, however, bemoaning the past. I could even regret that some poor devil would have to pay for killing Samuel Laing who had met no more than his just deserts. The main thing had been to clear my fiancée if it had been possible and at long last I saw a ray of hope.

"I suppose," said Guy at last, "that we ought to be congratulating ourselves that we've got the main problem out of the way. You must feel as though the world has suddenly become sane again, Mark," he smiled at me.

"Yes," I answered. "I feel that I can breathe again and that life can still have something beautiful in store for Veronica and me."

Guy looked at me intently.

"But remember, Mark," he said, "we're not yet out of the woods, you know that."

"Oh, I do realise that, Guy, but I feel just the same that it won't be too long when Veronica and I will be together again."

"You see, my friend," he went on, "what we've done is to establish a high probability that Veronica did not commit the crime. We haven't actually proved it, though I imagine we should get away with the case as it stands. At the same time, bearing everything in mind, there is still the possibility that the prosecution might contend that, as she was there and we can hardly deny it, she must have been an accessory to the crime."

"They would have to prove it."

"Yes. But don't forget that all policemen aren't like Dick Morris. They've got Veronica and they won't be too anxious to let her go unless they see that acquittal is absolutely inevitable. You don't know what other evidence might turn up. The vital thing as I see it, for us as well as the police, is to discover precisely what took place in that room and how Veronica came into it."

"Yes, I suppose it is important," I said sadly.

"Don't get so gloomy," Guy laughed. "It's not as bad as all that. It's my job to take all eventualities into account." He paused and then looked at me again. "I suppose you don't want to go on with the other ideas of yours now?" he asked. "It hardly seems necessary."

I shook my head. I had asked Guy to try and arrange a special visit for me so that I could submit Veronica to a kind of psychological investigation with a view to finding out her state of mind. "I don't think now, in the light of the new evidence, a psychological investigation would serve any purpose."

"Dick put the position rather neatly, I thought," Guy

went on, "when he said it was a case of having an eyewitness who could not see what happened."

"Yes, he did that very succinctly," I answered without much interest.

"All the same it's a pity we haven't some royal road of finding out what really happened in that room."

Guy said this with a rather curious intonation in his voice as though he were trying to make a suggestion.

"Yes, it would be of great help."

"I'll go and have a word tomorrow with the judge and the legal people for the prosecution," he said. "I must confess I'm not quite clear about our next best step. Whether to push forward with the trial and get an acquittal, or to make a petition for a free pardon on the basis of insufficient evidence. The free pardon is certainly attractive and Veronica will benefit by it. She and you, Mark, did have a great deal of undesirable publicity and a free pardon is always news. Though," he added bitterly, "knowing my British public I rather doubt it. They're firm believers in that rather dubious adage about no smoke without fire. In any case, there's that unsavoury story of her connection with Laing that none of us can explain away. Many will think the worst of that in any event."

Guy did not need to remind me of the position in which Veronica stood in the public estimation. Probably all her life there would be those heartless tormentors of the soul who would point her out and nod their heads, saying that she was the notorious Veronica Lloyd, the girl who got mixed up in that murder trial in 1976. And, of course ... Yes, that was the way they always went on. "Of course!" There was nothing more vile, to their minds, than that she would be acquitted.

"Is there anything more for me to discuss?" I asked abruptly. "It's been a very busy day and I didn't have much rest last night. I should like to turn in as soon as I can."

"No. I think the next moves lie with me." Guy stood up and held out his hand. "Sleep tight," he said. "Sorry I can't offer you a bed, but you know what these modern flats are. And thanks for your help, Mark. We can't be in much doubt now of the final outcome and we owe it all to your insight and rational reasoning."

I looked at him squarely. "I don't think I deserve your thanks, Guy," I replied. "I'm not very proud of having blundered in the early stages by not insisting to see the dagger and those photographs. We're lucky to have been able to do something at the eleventh hour. Well, I'll be pushing off."

"I'll ring you up tomorrow to report developments," he said. "Meantime, the main thought to trouble us is how we can establish exactly what took place in Laing's room. Perhaps Dick Morris will find out, but we mustn't overlook it just because the police have it in hand."

Once again there was the veiled hint of a suggestion in his words, but I was too tired to trouble about it. I was content, now the main problem had been solved, to let the morrow take care of itself.

Next morning I awoke with the impression that a great weight had been suddenly lifted from me, though for quite an appreciable time I could not think what it was. Then it burst upon me. Veronica was cleared. Immediately I sprang from my bed, feeling more energetic than I had been for some time.

As the morning wore on, however, this mood of elation slowly passed from me. There were still too many difficulties to be solved and Guy himself had been rather despondent about it all yesterday. The memory of my final talk with him came back to me. I suddenly recalled what I had taken to be his veiled hints. Whatever they were – if in fact, they did exist

– they were too thickly veiled for me to pierce the shroud of mystery. If my impression was right that he thought I could do something to help further to clear up the case, then he would have to be more specific.

It was getting on for noon when Guy rang and asked me if I could lunch with him. He seemed rather serious and I agreed to meet him at about one o'clock.

When I met him, his expression did nothing to raise my hopes again. He was looking dour and his greeting was distant. Indeed, it was not till we had finished our dessert that he deigned to say anything more than the vaguest commonplaces.

"Unfortunately, Mark," he said slowly, "there are more difficulties in the case than one had a right to expect. I don't know why but the police's attitude has altered – at any rate to some degree."

"Altered?" I repeated. "Do you mean they now refuse to help? Surely ..."

He checked me with a friendly gesture.

"No, not as bad as all that. But there are deeper waters running. They're not ready yet to help us get Veronica restored to the world."

"What the hell are you driving at, Guy?" I demanded. "Is there anything you're hiding from me?"

"Steady, Mark," he admonished. "Don't lose your temper, but just listen."

"Sorry, but you know my feelings about this," I said more calmly. "Please go ahead with your news."

"As I told you last evening, I went this morning and saw both the judge and the prosecution lawyers. They say that in their opinion the certainty of dismissal of the case or an acquittal cannot be taken for granted, in spite of the new turn of events. They all believe that the Crown would insist on a trial."

"But – but ..." I could not get the words out. This seemed to me incredible. "But surely, Guy," I said, calming myself, "that's unfair. We can prove that Veronica didn't commit the crime, even if she had been present at the scene of the murder. She was in a somnambulistic trance."

"That is not their view. Although Veronica, in the eyes of the law, is innocent until proved otherwise, the prosecution still thinks that there is sufficient ground for a trial." Guy paused for a moment. "You see, the weight of any fresh evidence must be sufficient, not simply to create an attitude of reasonable doubt in a jury's mind, but also to prove that the accused did not commit the murder. Can't you see the difference?"

"Yes. Though to me it's a typical piece of legal hair-splitting. I still think the evidence we've got is good enough."

He shook his head. "Apparently not. As we cannot bring proof that Veronica was not in the room at the material time, she is still the main suspect. According to the prosecution the only thing we've done is to show that the method of murder was different from that originally thought."

"But this is utterly stupid!" I cried. "Veronica couldn't have committed the crime!"

"Unfortunately, the experts believe that she could. None of us rejects the fact that she was there when Laing was killed. We can argue that the dagger with Veronica's fingerprints could not have been used for the murder because of the type of bloodstains and the particular fingerprints. On the other hand she confesses – and we do not dispute it – that she had murderous intentions against Laing. She could have had two knives and disposed of the one actually used, after dropping the other in the room."

I was thunderstruck. I had never imagined that legal niceties could be so completely insane. But Guy knew what he was talking about. It was, so he persisted, the view of the people who would handle the case for the Crown. It was a position almost as terrifying as the original one.

"You see," he went on, giving me a sympathetic glance, "the judges invariably tell juries that they are the sole judges of fact and that is a basic principle of English law. It is therefore necessary to protect that principle by every means."

"But that could be utterly unjust!" I burst out.

Again he checked me. "That may be so, but how can we prove it? The Crown will put forward the general view that though the details may be wrong, the broad outline is correct. So far the police have found no alternative murderer – perhaps they haven't looked for one yet, but that doesn't matter."

I gasped. "You don't mean that the authorities are ready to let an innocent woman suffer the indignity of a trial for a crime she didn't commit?"

Guy shook his head. "Quite definitely I don't. Like every other system the British system has its defects, but I do not believe for a moment that our police would leave any stone unturned in its task of solving the crime."

"Let's hope so," I said unconvincingly. "But surely you're not giving me a lecture on the working of our police?"

He smiled good-naturedly. "All lawyers tend to lecture," he replied. "What you have to remember is that every murder case is sifted and sifted again before the police are allowed to take it into Court. The attitude is that it is better on occasion to let a known murderer go free rather than try to get him convicted on insufficient evidence and run the risk of an acquittal which would do the police a lot of harm."

"But Veronica is not a murderer!" I objected. "This so-called attitude cannot surely apply to her?"

"No. Nobody's suggesting that she is. But we have to prove her innocence beyond a shadow of doubt. And that, my friend, could be very difficult in the circumstances."

"So it seems. And only this morning I thought the worst was over," I said bitterly. "But what can we do now? We can't do what the police haven't done – find the real murderer – like the great private detective in fiction."

"I wouldn't go so far as to say even that," he replied seriously. "The outsider often sees points that the professional overlooks, partly because his mind isn't biased and he's not troubled by the bane of orthodoxy. Besides you've not done so badly yourself in that line."

"Perhaps not, but one can't have that sort of luck all the time."

"There's no harm in trying," he said. I began to wonder again what he was driving at. Obviously he had something in mind, but for reasons of his own he would not tell me.

"So what do we do now?" I asked.

"Find out what the police are doing," he replied, signing to the waiter for his bill.

"We'll go round and see Inspector Morris. Thank heavens he's on the case. We must impress on him the urgency and seriousness we are in."

Shortly afterwards we left together in silence. There seemed little more to say. It looked to me as though the ray of hope I had seen had broadened into a flame and then died almost as quickly as it had appeared. I felt utterly deflated and the grave expression on Guy's face did nothing to lighten my feelings.

Dick Morris was not available when we telephoned Scotland Yard. So we left a message asking him to ring me as soon as he returned and then Guy and I parted. I went to my rooms in Harley Street and tried to busy myself with work, but it was of little use. Again and again my thoughts returned to this new crisis, all the worse because it had come when I had imagined the chief difficulty had been swept aside. I cursed the English law. I cursed the police. I even cursed Guy, though I did realise that all my thoughts were unfair. Guy was caught in the same net as I was and in a way his position was even more awkward, for he had to proceed with care since he was a part of the legal machine himself.

THIRTEEN

The day dragged on wearily without word from Dick. I returned to my home and told Maggie I wanted no dinner. If she brought me some toast and tea about half past seven, that would be quite sufficient. She began protesting, but I cut her short. She looked at me curiously but without resentment – she is accustomed to my moods by now – and went her way in silence.

It was past nine when Dick telephoned. I almost fell over myself in my eagerness to reach the instrument.

"I got your message, Mark," he said, "and I'd like to come round and see you right away."

"Why?" I asked puzzled. "Have you got some news?"

"Yes, I've news all right," he replied in a sort of tone that made my heart sink. "I'll tell you when I see you."

I telephoned Guy, who sounded as though he had been waiting as anxiously as I had. He agreed to come round at once and was at my door a good ten minutes before Dick put in an appearance. I saw from the first glance that his 'news', whatever it might be, was not likely to be good.

"It's been a hell of a day," he began, after draining in one gulp the drink I had given him.

Both Guy and I glanced questioningly at him.

"I was out on some work this morning – yes, part of the case," he went on. "This evening I've been to the worst conference I've ever attended. The Old Man, the D.P.P. himself and two or three officials from the H.O. A real field day!"

"Let's have it, Dick – the whole story," said Guy.

"I'll try and make a connected story of it, since I suppose it all links together," he answered Guy's prompting. "I had reviewed the whole case as though it were a fresh investigation, with the added difficulty that now the trail was cold and the bloke who had committed the crime had had plenty of time to get quite clear. But I wasn't down-hearted." He paused for a while.

Guy remained silent and I followed suit.

"I wasn't working quite on the lines the Old Man had indicated," Dick went on. "My line was simply this: Veronica hadn't done it; therefore someone else had. But who and how? So I went back and took another look at the premises. I'd got a couple of men with me and we had a good rake round the gardens. After about an hour's pretty thorough search we found something and I began to take hope."

"What was it?" I couldn't restrain myself of asking. If Dick had found something it meant the beginning of a new trail.

"I'll come to that, Mark," he replied, "in due course. I handed over my find to the experts for them to deal with and then I went to my desk. There was a note telling me about this conference. I was to bring with me the results of any work I had done so far. As there was little time left, I told the experts to get out an interim report and send it straight up to his office and I'd explain to the Old Man before we got to the conference."

"Didn't the Commissioner attend the conference?" asked Guy, while my whole being was quivering with eagerness to hear what it was that Dick had found.

Dick shook his head. "No. I promised to give him a detailed report. I did so – that's why I was so late in coming here. Well, I went into the Holy of Holies and found the whole lot assembled. There was Sir Eric Hoodman, the Director of Public Prosecutions, and a flaxen-haired, rabbit-faced chap I took to be his secretary.

Guy laughed, to Dick's obvious surprise. "Not a bad description of poor little Ambury," Guy said. "Don't forget, though, that his brains are inverse to his physical looks."

"I gathered that as things went along," said Dick. "Besides those two there was Tilman, from the Legal Department of the Home Office, and his assistant Burroughs."

Guy nodded. "I was talking to them this morning."

"That also I gathered as things went along," said Dick again. "And there was also Dr. Purfleet of the Lab. An imposing little lot."

"It shows the importance of the case in their eyes," commented Guy.

"Yes, I imagine it is important in the light of the new developments."

"For God's sake, Dick, get to the point!" I exclaimed, unable to stand this backchat any longer.

"All right, Mark. I understand your anxiety, old man."

"That's O.K." I said weakly. Obviously Dick was taking his time.

"From what I could understand, it's going to be pretty tough going, Guy," said Dick.

"So I gathered." Guy spoke precisely. "I saw Ambury this morning and one or two other people – unofficially, of course, and they told me the line they'd probably take. That's why we wanted to see you, Dick. We wanted to find out how the police investigation was proceeding."

Dick took a deep breath and then continued in a serious tone of voice.

"I'm not quite sure whether what we did discover would help our cause or not."

"Oh!" Guy appeared rather surprised. "What did you discover, Dick?"

"While searching the grounds round Laing's balcony, I found another knife buried beneath it."

So that was what he had found! I wondered why he had kept it back so long. He avoided my eyes as he resumed. Both Guy and I started forward in our chairs. Dick looked somehow uncomfortable and avoided our gaze.

"Yes," he went on, "it was a knife I'd found – and one which could have inflicted the fatal wound and not the dagger we discovered originally." Dick paused for a while and looked at us. "It was quite a find! Immediately I saw its implications. This obviously wasn't Veronica's knife and it would lead us a little nearer to the real culprit. Take a look at it, but be careful how you handle it."

He undid a small parcel he had carefully nursed all this time and exhibited the contents before us. It was a long narrow knife, very similar as regards the blade to that which had been found in Laing's room. There were old bloodstains on it too and the blade had rusted a little, no doubt from its long exposure. The handle, however, was of polished brown wood. It was the sort of weapon that many a sailor carries, especially those who have sailed in ships serving Eastern ports.

Once again my hopes rose and I saw that Guy too, seemed excited. This was the clue we were looking for! Dick, however, seemed not to share in our excitement.

"I told the bigwigs that this discovery put quite a new aspect on Veronica's case and they seemed to agree with me. All of us waited eagerly for the experts' report."

"Well?" Guy couldn't restrain his curiosity. "What did the experts find? Were there any fingerprints?"

Dick licked his lips and his words came like hammer blows to both Guy and myself.

"There were certainly fingerprints – a large number of confused prints. But there were three that were clearly marked, overlapping the other slightly indistinct impressions. These three fingerprints gave the impression they'd been made by someone gripping the knife very hard."

"Have those fingerprints been identified?" I cried, unable to restrain myself any further.

"Oh, yes, Mark," said Dick very slowly. "The prints were identified beyond any shadow of a doubt."

"Well, Dick?" Guy interrupted. "Whose fingerprints were they?"

"They were Veronica's," he answered in a barely audible voice.

"My God!" was all I could say. Then I sprang to my feet with a cry. The next I knew was that Guy was standing over me with a glass of water in his hand. The news that Dick revealed had struck me with the force of a physical blow and for a short moment I went right out. When I managed to pull myself together, I felt my head ringing and lights danced before my eyes. But this was no time for emotional storms. What was needed now was the clearest of clear thinking.

"Sorry, Dick," I muttered. "That was rather an unexpected shock. Please go on, let's hear the rest."

Dick cleared his throat. "It shattered me and the Old Man, too, as you can imagine." His mouth was thin and firm and he closed his eyes now and again – a habit of his when he is excited. But the mood quickly passed.

"I can understand what a blow this must be to you, Mark," he said quietly. "It was a hell of a shock to me too."

"There's no possibility of a mistake?" I asked stupidly. He shook his head slowly.

"And now what?" asked Guy in that calm, cold voice of his. "We have two knives, either of which could have inflicted the wound, but both bearing Veronica's fingerprints." He took a deep breath. "It looks to me," he began again, "as the Crown will point out, that the main picture is unchanged except in a few small details. The obvious inference would be that Veronica had two knives with her, that the one found in the room was dropped and that the actual killing was done with another knife, now discovered, which she threw away. I can't say that, on the face of it, it is at all an attractive case on which to hope for an acquittal or dismissal of the proceedings against Veronica."

"No," I said gloomily. "It looks as though we're back to square one. But I still can't believe that Veronica committed the murder!" I emphasised. "It is against all the probabilities of her personality."

"But that," observed Dick drily, "is one of those things which won't impress a Court. No, Mark, I don't say you're wrong even now. It is possible that again the known facts are being misinterpreted and that your belief is right. But that's not the sort of aspect we can argue very well in Court – is it, Guy?"

Guy shook his head. "Definitely, it is not!" he replied. "And we have to remember that we have less than a month to find something new that could bring an acquittal."

"Yes," Dick nodded sadly, "but in spite of the shocking new evidence, I'll continue with my routine investigation. I must admit, however, it looks pretty hopeless."

He looked at me as though expecting me to make some comment. But I remained silent. Now that this last-minute hope had been dashed to the ground, I had fallen into a mood of utter hopelessness. I couldn't see a single ray of light. The expected way out had proved not so much a cul-de-sac as a road leading in an even more damning indictment. I had expected either Guy or Dick to throw in their hands, but neither did. In fact, dull though my reactions were, I was really surprised to see that they seemed inclined to go on in a lost cause.

"Do you seriously entertain any hope at all?" I asked Dick at last.

He looked doubtful. "I admit, as I said before, I can't see any reasonable hope," he replied quietly. "The greatest tragedy is," he continued, "that Veronica is unable to give a really sound account of what happened. The truth is locked up in her somewhere, but behind a door to which we haven't the key. In fact, we can't find the key however hard we try."

"No," said Guy. "That is a very peculiar and arresting fact. But I suppose we have to accept it as it is. The only aspect to press upon at the trial has to be Veronica's psychological state. I doubt very much," he concluded, "that any fresh facts will come to light between now and the trial."

"And there I suppose we'd better leave it. I don't see that we can get any further now," I said wearily. "To me the whole thing looks utterly hopeless and the more we talk the more hopeless it seems. I'm really grateful to you both for your loyalty ..."

Dick held up his hand. "Don't put it that way, Mark," he said sincerely. "It's not a matter of loyalty but rather that both of us believe, deep in our hearts, that you're right. The stumbling block is that we can't find the proof. I shall feel an utter failure if I don't get some kind of a new line on this case. I shall do my damnedest anyway."

Guy nodded and rose to his feet. "Mark," he said, "I'm only a lawyer and you're a doctor, but I'm going to give you some advice. For God's sake take something tonight to make you sleep. You look on the verge of a collapse and if you pack up that may mean the end of our last hope of success. Remember that the worst service you could do to Veronica would be to let your worries get on top of you. You do see that, don't you?"

"Yes," I said dully. "Though I don't see that I've done anything useful so far, except to make things blacker than they might have been."

He gripped my hand and looked me full in the eyes, but he said no more. A few minutes later they left me and I was alone once more with surely the heaviest thoughts any man ever had.

FOURTEEN

There was no more news for me the next day until late in the evening when Guy called on me unexpectedly. I had remained at home, partly for being immediately available should I be needed and partly because I felt too lethargic to do anything else but sit and brood. I was hardly following Guy's well-meant advice not to let the anxiety get on top of me. But I knew from experience that it is almost impossible for anybody in a state of psychological gloom to keep a rational course. Many a time had I given patients advice that I knew they could not carry out.

Guy gave me an appraising look when he came in.

"You don't look too good," he remarked when he had refused the drink I offered him. "Keep a tight hold on yourself, Mark, and remember what I said last night."

"I know, Guy, that your advice was meant well," I replied sadly. "But if you were a doctor you'd know how difficult it is to follow any advice, no matter how good. But I'm doing my best. Anyway, what brings you here? Is there any new development?"

He smiled a little grimly. "I'm here partly because I wanted to see you, but mostly because I feel you need a friend to be near you, Mark," Guy said quietly. "It's no good brooding day and night. You'll turn yourself into a nervous wreck. You doctors never know how to look after yourselves, any more than we lawyers can make our own wills. But I also wanted to report on what I've been doing, though it's not too much, I'm afraid."

"I'm glad, Guy, you came," I smiled. "Whatever news you bring it can't be worse than what we already know. To tell the truth, I would almost welcome the news that it was all over."

"Steady, Mark." Again those words which had helped me so much before. He had an air of unshakeable stability when he spoke them and I felt grateful to him for that.

"Yes, Guy," I said. "I admit I was going a bit haywire. Psychologists have been known to go nuts too, you know!" I laughed for the first time that day. It felt strange but good. "What's your news?"

He gave me a sympathetic look. "I've had another busy day," he answered. "This knife business was something which, I felt, should be cleared up, so I asked for an immediate interview with Veronica. As you can guess, officialdom moves slowly, but I managed to get the permit almost at once and I went down to see her."

"Oh, Guy," I cried eagerly. "How – how IS she?"

"As well as can be expected. She looks a bit drawn and tired, of course," he told me gently, "but she seems to be remarkably calm. I think, Mark, that Veronica is the most courageous woman I've ever met." He paused for a moment. "That is one reason why I'm determined to do my utmost for her even though it might break me!" he almost shouted.

"Thanks, Guy," I said. "You'll never know how much good this's doing me."

"I told her everything that had happened, including the finding of the knife," he went on, brushing off my thanks. "She stared at me in a sort of surprise. Quite obviously the news astonished her and when I asked her if she had ever had a knife of that kind, she replied with a very definite 'NO'.

There was no hesitation before she replied and I'm experienced enough to know when a witness is lying. My firm belief is that Veronica knows nothing about that second knife."

"That's something, but where does it get us?"

"Not far, I'm afraid," Guy continued. "Veronica was in a somnambulistic trance, we're assuming, and so might easily do things of which she has no memory whatever. On the other hand, she may not have had a second knife, but it's conceivable that she found it in the room and used it. So, I'm afraid, the prosecution would insist. So, where does that get us?"

"Nowhere, it seems," I replied. "That damn sleep-walking business complicates matters."

"It does, most decidedly. I found that out rather later when I had an interview with Sir James Shelsdon."

"The H.O. pathologist?" I asked in some surprise. He was most likely the man who would be called upon to give medical evidence for the Crown. I looked at Guy questioningly.

"You seem surprised," he returned, "but I wanted a really authoritative ruling on a point that had occurred to me. Sir James is, I believe, one of our foremost medico-legal experts, isn't he?"

I nodded. "Yes. He's that, but ..."

"Good," Guy checked me. "I had to be convinced that Veronica could not have inflicted the fatal wound even if she did own the second knife. We had formed the opinion that the wound was deep and needed far more strength for its execution than Veronica possessed. So I went and asked Shelsdon's opinion."

"What did he say?" I asked.

"He'd had the whole facts of the case sent to him for review," Guy answered, "so he knew all about it and had come to the conclusion that she could have committed the crime."

"But how on earth ...?"

"Just because of that somnambulism," replied Guy. "Apparently Shelsdon has examined Veronica and knows a good deal about her physical condition. His opinion is that in a normal state, Veronica could hardly have had the strength to inflict such a wound, but there were certain conditions in which it might be possible for her."

"What conditions?" I asked.

"Well, such as her being in a somnambulistic trance and the fact that Laing was knifed in his sleep," Guy emphasised. "He said it was an established fact that sleep-walkers are capable of many things during their excursions that would be physically impossible for them in a waking state, including the exercise of exceptional strength."

"Very clever of him," I commented bitterly. "Though it seems to me to be putting the cart before the horse. He's taking for granted that she actually committed the murder and then adjusting the circumstances to uphold his assumption?"

"You can put it that way, if you like, and it does really represent the position. We must never forget that she admitted to being in a trance and to the likelihood that she did kill Samuel Laing." Guy stressed the point. "The only way to get her out of that mess is to prove that she did not kill Laing, in spite of her admission." He paused for a while and looked at me. "And so far none of the facts we've established are of any help to us. On the contrary, they are consistent with the conception that she did the killing. I must admit that the outlook gets less and less hopeful."

I sighed. "It does look like that. Yet I still say two things. One is that the whole thing is inference, and the second is Veronica's personality."

"That, unfortunately, applies to almost every murder trial. The evidence is more often than not circumstantial and the verdict rests on a probability that excludes reasonable doubt."

"Yes, I know that," I rejoined. "But I still maintain that murder is inconsistent with her personality and the chances of her committing one in a somnambulistic trance are even more remote than of her doing it in her waking hours."

Guy shook his head. "That's a specialist's view you will never get the ordinary man in the street and much less the lawyer, with his distrust of scientific opinion, to accept."

He put his hand on my shoulder. "Be honest, Mark," he said. "You'd be the last man to contend that we know all there is to know about human personality or the human mind. We've got to face it though your view may be a very sound one, this – Veronica's case – may be the exception to an otherwise general rule. Isn't that so?"

I had argued that point again and again with myself. "Yes, I accept that," I replied wearily.

I wondered whether he was on the point of abandoning all hopes. Guy seemed to read my thoughts.

"It was a hard thing to say, Mark," he went on softly, "but it had to be said. I shall go on with the case, but I confess that unless Dick Morris brings in something startling, it looks – well, it looks lost to me. Believe me, Mark, if it were the last case in my career, I couldn't wish more for a happy outcome. Unfortunately the facts speak for themselves and it'll be little short of a miracle if they could be upset now. The only hope lies now in a psychological theory. If that can be proved, it might lead to the end we all want. But can it, Mark – can it? That's your line of country."

He scrutinized me with a look that held in it a suggestion of an appeal. I shook my head doubtfully.

"I don't know," I replied. "Frankly, I don't feel capable of trusting anybody or anything, least of all myself."

Guy rose and held out his hand.

"Have a last shot, old man," he said. "It's your last chance – and Veronica's."

FIFTEEN

I was not left long alone with my despondent thoughts. Barely half an hour after Guy had left me, my housekeeper came in to say that Inspector Morris wished to see me.

"Please, show him in, Maggie," I said.

"Yes, Master Mark." She smiled at me and went out of the room.

He seemed in a very distracted mood, which was quite unusual for the normally calm and self-possessed man I knew him to be. As he sat down on one of the armchairs in the room, I noticed that his face bore an expression very similar to that which Guy had worn on his departure. It suggested that he, too, was facing defeat after a long and arduous battle in which everything had gone against him.

For some little time Dick sat staring at the floor, as though brooding over the way in which he should begin an unpleasant talk.

"Well, Dick?" I asked, trying to calm myself. "What's the news from your end of the business?"

My tone was rather brusque but he did not seem to notice the fact. His placidity did nothing to reassure me.

"Heard from Guy?" he asked, apparently evading a direct answer to my question.

I told him about Guy's visit and his misgivings about the outcome of Veronica's case. When I had finished, he nodded as though what I had said was merely confirmation of what he already suspected.

"It's not too good, is it?" he commented. "Is Guy still willing to go on with the case?"

"Yes," I answered, "he's going to see it through, but I think he's practically abandoned hope. His view is that the only real chance lies in my proving my own psychological theories. That may be all right for me, but I doubt whether I could ever convince either the judge or the jury."

"True enough," he returned. "If it's got to that stage, then there's little more to be said."

Dick made a slight movement as though about to get up without saying anything of the reason for his visit. But I checked him. If he had come to see me, it must be for some purpose and it was unlike Dick to run away from a task, however unpleasant.

"What is it you came here to tell me, Dick?" I asked.

He hesitated. "It's barely worth talking about," he replied. "My results have been quite negative."

I gave him a keen glance. "Now look here, Dick," I said. "Just what is biting you? You didn't come here just to tell me that. Why are you stalling? It isn't like you, Dick. If you have bad news I would like to hear it. I've had so many shocks lately that one more wouldn't make any difference."

He looked me in the face squarely for the first time since his arrival in my home.

"I'm sorry, Mark," he replied at long last. "The whole mess has troubled me a great deal and as Guy and yourself appeared to have given up hope, I couldn't bring myself to give you more bad news."

"I appreciate your concern, Dick," I said firmly. "I want to know everything, no matter how bad it is. Don't gloss over anything, please!"

"O.K.," he said and paused for a moment. "Well, it's like

this. As I went through the dossier again, I began to realise that we'd made a sorry mess of the original investigation. There were all sorts of things I ought to have done but omitted just because there was so much proof on hand." He paused again. "Everyone was so impressed by the existing evidence that they thought no further corroboration was necessary."

"You needn't reproach yourself for that, Dick," I said in all sincerity. "We are all to be blamed for taking everything for granted."

"Oh yes, I do blame myself for going straight to Veronica and there my routine inquiries ended. I thought I saw more than enough to satisfy myself, yet I saw nothing. The imaginative witness, Mark, is the curse of the police."

"I can't see what else you could have done in the circumstances," I answered puzzled. I could not see what he was driving at.

"Oh yes," he said firmly. "A lot of things."

"For instance?"

"I should have looked for a lead elsewhere – I mean a lead that meant inquiries in other quarters and not stopping at Veronica's door."

"Perhaps you could have done that, Dick," I said. "But is it too late to start now?"

"No," he answered. "That's exactly what I and my men have been doing."

"Well? Any success?"

"At first – none. We found one or two people who had seen a light in Laing's room and we got more dope on Laing's nasty habits. His usual callers too were quite an unsavoury bunch. Particularly one of them – a certain Giacomo Albertini, an Italian. Nobody we questioned seemed to know exactly who Giacomo was, except that he was Laing's right-hand man."

"So, finally you discovered the mystery man. Pity the Press missed that," I put in sarcastically.

"A good story, but nothing much in it," Dick continued.

"Did you manage to trace this Giacomo Albertini?"

"Oh, yes. We tracked him down, living in a charming little house just outside Esher. It was quite a revelation seeing the luxuries he was surrounded with. At first he wasn't prepared to talk but we managed to make him spill the beans. Yes, our Giacomo had been in Laing's flat at almost the exact hour, so far as we could gather. On his way to see Laing, Giacomo told us, he was surprised to see a light in his room because he knew how much Laing hated resting in a room with the lights on."

"Go on." I felt that a blow was coming, but I couldn't help being interested.

"Then Signor Albertini got a further surprise. The windows were wide open and he stopped walking for a moment wondering what had happened. And then something did happen."

I saw Dick's brow covered with sweat – a very unusual event – and his fingers began to fidget a little. I braced myself for the coming shock.

"Yes," he went on, "Giacomo saw something all right. While he was watching, a figure came out on the balcony. He could see it quite plainly because of the light streaming out." Dick's sentences became jerky. "It was the figure of a woman in a dressing gown. He thought of Veronica because he knew something about her relations with Laing. And then he saw the woman throw an object over the edge into the bushes below. Giacomo says he saw it flash. Then caution overcame him and he bolted. In other words he saw Veronica throw away the knife."

I was dumbfounded. All things seemed to conspire against Veronica. "My God, what next?" I cried in despair.

I turned my face towards my friend. "Do you believe his story, Dick?"

Dick nodded. "At first, I didn't. But he told us that the object Veronica threw out suggested a knife to him and that was why he ran. Giacomo said there were quite a few people willing to do Laing in if the chance came and he didn't want to get mixed up with trouble. That sounded plausible and as I hadn't mentioned the knife to him, if it was invention it was a very remarkable coincidence. I made a note of what he'd said, but didn't take it too seriously – then. I was inclined to believe he had romanticised it a little."

"But something more turned up?" I insisted.

Again Dick nodded slowly.

"Unfortunately yes, Mark." He began his tale again. "When I got back to Central, I found Sergeant Collins waiting for me. You see, I had asked him to do some investigation on his own. He told me what he'd found out."

"Go on, Dick, please!" I implored.

"Well, Collins discovered someone on the other side of the road who'd been attracted by the light from Laing's flat and had stood watch out of curiosity. He, too, had seen the woman on the balcony throwing something over the rail, though he couldn't say what it was. There was corroboration enough. But the man went further. He had gone out on his own balcony to have a closer look – perhaps he's the sort that a vision of a woman in a dressing gown interests – and he'd heard a noise and he'd seen someone dashing off down the street. That may or may not have been Giacomo, but it squares up. Anyway we've two witnesses that Veronica threw something into the bushes where we found the knife. It looks to me like something we can't get round."

I felt the calmness I had experienced during Dick's narrative ebbing from me. The world was growing black as midnight again. Nausea rose in me, but I managed to fight it down. It was the last nail in Veronica's coffin. What could we do now? I braced myself and looked steadily at Dick.

"You think this is the end?" I asked.

He rose to his feet with an effort. Slowly he returned my gaze. "What else can I think, Mark? The more we unearth, the more the proof piles up. It's hopeless. I'd like to think otherwise, but what else is there to think? What other conclusion can we come to than that Veronica murdered Laing? It's inevitable, Mark. Believe me, I did try hard hoping to find some loopholes and found nothing. I can't do anything more, my friend – really I can't. Have pity on me! I've got to believe that Veronica murdered Laing. Whether she was walking in her sleep or not, I don't know. But she did it. She knows she did it. I don't judge her. Laing was a rotter. But the fact remains that he was murdered."

I put my hand on his shoulder.

"Dick," I said, as calmly as I could. "Don't blame yourself. Nobody could have done more. You've made a real fight and done more than any other man in your position would have done. I'm not blaming you – nobody is! On the contrary I'm grateful to you because you put friendship first and did so willingly. No man could do more than that. You've risked your whole career and reputation just to help us, and that I can never repay. I don't reproach you or criticize you, so don't reproach or criticize yourself and Veronica would be the last to think ill of you. Thanks, Dick, not only for what you've done but also for telling me all this so frankly. It'll be over soon and then we can all try to forget."

"I wish I could think so," he murmured. "I don't think I shall ever forget these days of hell, when all I've been doing is sending a friend – a woman friend at that – to prison for life and all through trying to help her."

"I, too, won't ever be able to forget, Dick." I tried to help him get over his depression. "Think of me, my friend. Think of my life without Veronica! It's too dreadful even to contemplate."

"I know, Mark. I can guess how lonely you'll be without the woman you love so dearly. I know and am worried like hell!"

I grasped his hand.

"Don't worry, Dick. You've been marvellous. And if it's any consolation to you – Veronica and I really are and always will be grateful to you – no matter what happens."

He gave me a quick glance, pressed my hand and almost stumbled from the room. It was the first and last time I was ever to see Dick Morris the victim of his own emotional stress. He was, at that moment, a broken, bitterly disappointed man – perhaps more broken and disappointed than I was, if that was at all feasible. It was a far from pleasant sight and it is one I shall never forget – though never to his discredit. He had played a noble and self-sacrificing part in the whole affair. Without Dick Morris, the case would have been even more disastrous.

SIXTEEN

The desire for oblivion was no longer with me. Dick's visit had altered that. There was, it was true, no new problem to face. He had added merely one more confirmation to the mass of proof that had already been put before me. The cruel hard fact had to be faced. Say what he might, Guy was now convinced that Veronica had killed Samuel Laing. He might pretend that he believed my psychological theory of the case, but as a practical, keen-minded lawyer, he knew that the situation was hopeless and I was quite prepared to hear from him that he had decided to abandon all hopes of an acquittal. Dick Morris, the clearest-minded detective-officer in Scotland Yard, had been forced to arrive at the same conclusion in spite of himself. They both saw Veronica now as a murderess. Whether she had been in a somnambulistic trance or not at the time did not matter very much to either, for each brought his own professional viewpoint to bear, however he might protest that he did not. To Guy, the lawyer, the case was hopeless. He was more concerned, after all, with the legal position and the legal attitude, than with questions of absolute truth and proof. No Court under the British Crown could decide otherwise than that Veronica was a murderess; and that sort of conclusion was the type by which he regulated his life.

Dick Morris was essentially the policeman. He had

expressed the view quite early in the case that Samuel Laing was the sort of man who might well be obliterated, without loss to the community. But his attitude towards murder as a policy was unchanged. As a police officer, he hated murder. His job was to see that the peace was kept and that disputes between citizens were kept within bounds. If anyone was allowed to take to killing for private ends, no matter what the justification in the abstract, the whole fabric of society would break down into gangsterdom. He might seek facts as conscientiously as he knew how; he might rest content with nothing but the strongest proof; but in the long run the killer was his enemy, his quarry, no matter who he might be. And if the fact of killing was established beyond any shadow of a doubt, he would do nothing to help the culprit.

They were both still my friends. They had given more to me for Veronica's sake than I had any right to expect. Yes, they both had gone to the extreme limits of friendship for me and had not admitted defeat till the event was inescapable. I could have no quarrel with them. I was conscious even at that, my blackest hour, of an intense and warm gratitude for their unremitting efforts, which had not been without cost to either of them. If I must lose Veronica, I had what compensation I might be able to find in the thought of two staunch and unselfish friends. I must admit that then, as I sat thinking after Dick's departure, I did not derive much comfort from the thought.

The proof was sufficient now to convince not only the authorities and the Courts of Veronica's guilt, but also these two loyal supporters and fellow-workers. It should have convinced me also. But even then, when the last word seemed to have been spoken, I still could not believe it. That Veronica could have killed anyone was to me as impossible as anything else in the world.

I thought of her as I have always known her. A hundred

and one little incidents crowded in on me. Not one of them carried the faintest suggestion that within her was the violent passion of the woman who kills in rage or the cold, calculating drive of the one who slays by design. For that was a point that had to be squarely faced; and as I reached that point in my thoughts I realised that it never had been squarely faced, at any rate by me, who was supposed to have a complete psychological theory of the case.

The point was this: that however the murder was supposed to have been committed by Veronica, whether in her sleep-walking or when she had been awake and in full possession of her senses, it was a murder by design. The idea of hot anger flaming into a sudden murderous impulse could not be entertained for a single instant. Here was Samuel Laing sleeping the sleep, if not of the just, at any rate that of a tired and busy man, lying peacefully on his divan in an interval between his curious hours of business. While he was thus, the theory was that Veronica came to him armed with a knife or knives and struck the fatal blow, not in panic, but with tremendous strength and what seemed either astonishing luck or something more than a superficial knowledge of human anatomy. If Veronica had done it in her sleep, then it must be that she had planned every detail of it with a thoroughness that was astonishing. The other alternative was that she had designed it and executed it while fully awake.

The more I thought about it, the less believable the whole thing seemed. Understanding her position and knowing what she had done by purchasing that knife, she had tried to explain everything as well as she could; but there had never been the slightest hint of deliberate planning in detail such as the actual crime exhibited. I felt sure that she would have mentioned it, if only to me. And knowing Veronica as I do, I felt sure that she would have given herself away to Guy in his keen questioning of her to get at the true facts. She was as fogged as any of us on the actual details.

There was, of course, one other possibility. She might be so cold and calculating, so devoid of human feelings, that she had deliberately concealed the planning and hoped by this fake confession to gain a clemency that would otherwise have been denied her. Again my knowledge of Veronica told me that that idea was so fantastic that it could occur only to a man in so parlous a mental and emotional state as I was. She simply could not play a part like that. She believed that she had murdered Laing in a state of somnambulism. But she knew nothing more; and, as Guy had said, practically all the details she had given were after suggestions, the result of what she had been told about the discovery of the footprints, the knife and the fingerprints.

The contradiction was almost too big to be true and yet it was there and had to be accepted. On the one hand was Veronica's character, which was neither violent nor unstable; on the other were incontrovertible facts which, the more they multiplied, pointed ever more conclusively in the direction of her guilt. It was almost as though we were dealing with two different people, both with the physical characteristics of Veronica. I could not and would not attempt even explaining the turmoil in my brain.

At this stage I found myself thinking of the principle of the dialectics, with which our Hegelian and Marxist philosophers make so much play. Here, truly enough, were two opposites in acute contradiction, so much so that all hope of reconciliation between them was practically unthinkable. Yet I did not dare then to hope that the dialectic principle was right and that out of these opposites a greater, combining resolution of truth would come. They seemed irreconcilable beyond the most determined logic-chopping.

For all that, I began a series of speculations within my own province. I myself am no logician, except in the sense that every worker in a scientific field has to work to logical principles and be able to draw deductions and make inferences from observed facts. But I do claim to know something of my own sphere and the idea of the two Veronicas in contradiction to each other, brought to my mind a possibility I had never before considered in this connection.

The psychiatrist is only too familiar with the schizophrenic, the person who is two personalities in one. He knows that the fantasy of Jekyll and Hyde is the commonplace of the neurotic world. Split personality, to some degree, is a very common thing and by no means the exotic rarity some people imagine it to be.

Yet schizophrenia, even in its mildest form, has its signs, which the psychiatrist usually has little difficulty in recognizing. They may not always, at first sight, indicate schizophrenia, but they do advertise clearly neurotic tendencies of some kind.

I racked my brain for any such symptoms in Veronica. I had known her for a not inconsiderable time. I had been on terms of great intimacy with her, seen her almost daily, gone out with her, spent quiet evenings and nights with her. Never once had my professional interest been aroused with her and I felt pretty certain that if she had shown the slightest trace of a neurotic symptom I should have noticed it, for I am one of those uncomfortable people for whom work is never far away. Even more perhaps than the physician, the psychiatrist has to be constantly on the alert for the smallest tell-tale signs from his patients and noticing them is a habit one can never entirely lose even in one's moments of relaxation. That Veronica should be neurotic without my having observed a single thing was too much for me to believe. Nor was my lack of belief in the possibility due entirely to professional pride. I realised that I had consciously and deliberately studied Veronica, without her being aware of it, for such signs.

No, Veronica was definitely not a schizophrenic. I knew that in any case it would have made no difference to the legal position. But I was not satisfied for all that. For my own peace of mind and still more to re-establish Veronica's integrity, I was determined that by one means or another I must find out the real truth.

For a long time I sat thinking in my chair with a growing sense of calm. The blow had fallen, but was it really the final blow? And just as before, when that last word appeared to have been said and all that remained was waiting for the end, I had felt a sudden spurt of confidence and purpose, so now my resolution grew till it swept away the last traces of my deadly depression.

I suppose I ought not to confess that I slept well that night. Naturally I was glad I was able to get some sleep, natural sleep. It was the result of that confidence which had come to me that evening and a sign that I had again got a grip on myself. Not that I had come to any line of practical action. I was as far from seeing daylight amid the fog of my problems as ever. Yet I did not try to force myself to 'face facts' – a phrase which all too often means simply bowing to the force of external circumstances. The Victorian belief that man is only man when he is being a rational animal, is dead. Modern psychology has discovered that man is ruled at least as much by irrational impulses as by rational ones and the psychiatrist would be the last to say that an inner conviction based on apparently no logical premise is any less real or important in a man's life than a conclusion reached by the most stringent and exhaustive of logical arguments. My confidence was based on such an inner conviction and it gave me courage in the face of difficulties that might otherwise have overwhelmed me – as in fact they very nearly had already.

The morning brought with it no immediate relief. Guy telephoned to say that Dick Morris had been to see him early and told him what he had told me. The case was now, in Guy's opinion, quite hopeless from the legal point of view. He asked me to review the case in the light of these developments and give him my decision whether I wanted to let the trial take its course. I told him I would think the matter over.

He seemed surprised at the calmness with which I spoke, but I did not enter into details with him. For I was, now I came to think of it, filled with a new hope and determination. Veronica must be cleared. She could be cleared. I was certain of it – almost more so than before. My own theory, based on some little experience, is that convictions of this kind are due to the fact that the unconscious, with its utter timelessness, has seen the solution of a problem before the conscious has grasped it. Also I believe convictions arise from a leakage of information from the unconscious to the conscious level. In time, the whole solution emerges from the unconscious and the inner conviction is justified. In my case, I had the distinct impression that a fresh light was about to break and I was content to let it work its own way without trying to force it – an effort that might easily repress it beyond reach.

Again I began to consider the possibility of Veronica being a schizophrenic. In particular I asked myself whether her somnambulism was not some sort of evidence of a neurotic trend. It was not the first time I had done so, but once again I decided that it was not. It was just an intense form of dreaming. Dreaming is not a sign of neurotic tendencies, since it is a safety valve for the unconscious and it is only when that safety valve is overloaded that signs of danger may be detected in the dream. In so far as sleep-walking enabled her to work off her repressed wishes, it was perhaps an aid to her normality. Veronica's somnambulism, as it stood, was not an evidence of either neurosis or of schizophrenia in particular.

So the morning passed without anything definite emerging. I lunched at home, still with the feeling that something would occur to me soon and in the early afternoon I telephoned Guy to say that I left the course of the trial entirely in his hands. He was to act as his judgement suggested. Once again he seemed surprised.

"What's happening, Mark?" he asked. "You seem damned off-hand about it."

"There's nothing to get excited about, is there?" I returned. "The result of the trial can't alter things very much, whichever way it goes. I've just taken myself in hand as you told me I must."

Guy chuckled. "That's a very neat way of getting your own back," he said. "The perfect professional retort to the amateur. All the same I'm glad to hear you're feeling better. You really worried me when I last saw you."

"I'm glad to feel better myself," I replied.

It was towards evening when I was first struck by the idea – the idea that had been working its way up from the unconscious ever since the previous night. That is the only explanation I can give of the fact that then, without any specific object in view, I began almost desultorily to turn to my reference shelves and consult some authorities on somnambulism and hypnotism. My library is, of its kind, very complete and I was able to consult with both old and modern writers on the subject. And from this seemingly chance reading, though I am sure myself it was unconsciously motivated, came the plan for action.

The scheme at first looked fantastic enough. Not only was its success doubtful on purely scientific grounds; there were obstacles in the way that to me looked insuperable. To overcome those alone, I would need all the help Guy and his friends could offer. Another aspect of the matter struck me with such force that it was almost breathtaking.

Time and again I had felt that Guy was trying to suggest a course of action to me without putting it into specific terms. At that last dismal interview with him he had said frankly that the last hope lay with me because of my background. Could it be that he had vaguely sensed that I could help in some such way as now occurred to me? It seemed unlikely, for he was only a layman, yet often the outsider sees things which the professional overlooks. Perhaps that was why he had been so vague – a thing he usually avoided. It might be that he had seen the main problem to be psychological and therefore mine, but had been unable to put the idea into any reasonable form of words.

That thought was encouraging, but I realised, of course, that I might easily be deceiving myself and trying to explain away an uncomfortable difficulty. I did not think so, however. The whole idea that Guy making vague suggestions to me might easily be a figment of my own imagination could not be dismissed. But as I thought back on it I was convinced that that was not so. Guy expected me to act in some way or other and he would be grievously disappointed in me if I did not.

It was, therefore, with a much lighter heart than I might have expected that I dialled my friend's number. He was out, much to my disappointment. I left a message that I wanted to speak to him urgently and asked his clerk to pass it on to his home, if necessary, so that he should not miss it. The clerk promised to do so and I had to be content with that.

I was having dinner when Guy rang, apologizing for having been unable to ring before. In my turn I apologized for being a nuisance.

"I want you to come round as soon as you can," I begged. "I've got an idea I want to discuss with you."

He showed no surprise. He did not even press me for some explanation of my request. There was almost a note of relief in his voice as though this was something for which he had been waiting.

"I'll be round as soon as I've had a bite to eat," he said cheerfully.

SEVENTEEN

Guy came to my house sooner than I expected. Less than half an hour had passed when I heard my door bell ringing. Soon after, Maggie led him directly to my lounge.

"So you've got a fresh idea, Mark," he said, as he settled himself and lit his pipe. "I can't tell you how glad I am that you have. I was beginning to think we'd seen the end of all this unfortunate affair."

"You didn't want it to be the end?"

He shrugged his shoulders. "Most certainly not. For one thing, I hate leaving a case with an ending I consider unsatisfactory. For another, I do not like to give my friends the impression that I'm deserting them at the last moment."

"You needn't worry about the second point, Guy," I returned. "I never thought of you as quitting and I'm sure Veronica never would. So you think the end you visualized would have been unsatisfactory?"

"Certainly," he replied. "I think I am almost as convinced as you are that this case is a hopeless muddle with all the signposts pointing in the wrong direction. I have even played with the idea," he continued with a slight smile, "that it was the perfect murder – so dear to detective book novelists – planned by someone with a friendly precise design to fix it inescapably on Veronica. But I soon rejected that notion. The very idea was fantastic. No. I came to the conclusion some time ago that it was a curious combination of chances which, though trivial in themselves, multiply together till they give an overwhelming probability, which is in itself the greatest possible travesty of the truth."

"You mean, then, that you have never considered Veronica guilty – not even these past two days?"

He shook his head apologetically. "To my shame, Mark," he confessed, "I began to consider her guilty, particularly after the new evidence Dick Morris unearthed, but that feeling passed quickly."

"Why, Guy?" I asked. "What made you change your belief in Veronica's guilt?"

"Both of you, but mostly Veronica herself." He paused for a moment. "I soon returned to my original opinion that she was incapable of murder and the more I thought about it the more convinced I became," he went on. "My reasons for thinking that were not, perhaps, the same as yours. You knew Veronica better than anyone else involved and besides you base your opinions on professional experience. But in a different way, I too, am a pretty good judge of character especially in regard to the commission of crime. I felt that Veronica was not lying but telling the truth as she thought she saw it. Her one belief was that she had killed Samuel Laing while she was sleep-walking and she accepted everything that was put to her as an explanation."

"Yet all that might be true," I said, "and she could still be guilty on the sleep-walking theory."

Guy shook his head again. "No. There I was convinced by your arguments," he replied. "You, Mark, had ample authority to back you and what you said seemed irrefutable."

"I'm glad you did take me seriously," I commented.

"I began to form an opinion that the only way to get to the bottom of the matter and unravel it was to use psychological means. But I am the merest tyro in psychology. I hadn't the faintest notion what could be done and it would have been sheer impertinence on my part to make suggestions to you."

I smiled grimly. "But you dropped a few hints, didn't you?"

"Yes, I did. But I wasn't sure that you'd taken them, even when, the other evening, I was more definite than I had ever been." Guy went on, "I even considered the idea of coming out into the open but decided against it because there was always the chance that Dick might unearth some fresh fact that would annul all the other deductions. Unfortunately he didn't. The further he went, the blacker affairs grew. On purely evidential grounds, the case against Veronica would be absolutely damning."

He paused and slowly re-lit his pipe.

"Before you tell me, Mark, what you've got in mind," Guy said, "I'd like to run through the case as it stands today. It will be familiar to you, of course – too familiar, probably, but I want to show you why I decided it had come to the stage when you alone could do something to help."

I nodded my head. And as he went on recounting over and over again all the evidence we'd had so far, I began to wonder why he was bringing out again all these familiar facts, yet I saw one good thing in it: I had never before realised how utterly damning this evidence was and the impossibility of refuting it by any ordinary defence.

"Yes," he went on, "if with all the additional facts available, we had put up the defence of sleep-walking, I think we would be torn to shreds. I mean, the prosecution will bring out all the things I mentioned. Perhaps it's as well that things turned out as they did. And now shall we hear what you have to say?" he ended, looking at me with fresh interest.

All I can say, after telling Guy about my theory, is that he seemed impressed not only by my proposals, but also by the formidable obstacles that stood in the path of their realisation.

For a little while, after having made a general remark of agreement, he sat silently smoking, as though turning the whole affair over in his mind.

"Yes," he said at last, "I suppose it was something of this kind I had in my mind when I dropped those hints to you, though I never thought of it in such definite terms. It'll be a hell of a job, Mark, you realise that. We shall have to break down every precedent on record. I wonder what's the best way to begin?"

"I'd played with the idea of going to Sir George again and trying to enlist his help," I suggested.

Guy pondered for a moment and then shook his head. "No," he said, "I don't think that would be wise. He's been very decent to us and we mustn't presume on it. Besides I don't think this is up his street. You see, he was anxious that the truth of the case should be established. He told Dick Morris to do his utmost to get additional facts. Dick has done that but the facts, as he thinks, have confirmed the original findings. Sir George will be satisfied with that. No, I think that, except as a last resort, Sir George Poole is out. That goes for Dick Morris too. We must not forget that Dick is a policeman and he has to think in police terms. No, Mark. This calls for other and more devastating measures."

He relapsed into thought again.

"We mustn't outrage officialdom at the outset and so create unnecessary difficulties for ourselves," Guy went on at last. "First, I shall make an application through the usual channels. No doubt they'll ask the reason for such an entirely new step and I shall reply that I'd give the necessary details at the highest level. That, I think, will short-circuit the prison service officials, who are not exactly progressive or adventurous in their outlook."

"Won't all that take time?" I asked dubiously.

"No doubt it will, but it's not all I propose to do. I shall call at the Old Bailey and try to speak to Judge Falkirk."

"Judge Falkirk?" I queried. "The judge in charge of the case?"

"Precisely. If I can see him – and I think I can – I hope to be able to convince him that we are acting in the best interests of justice."

"I hope so. That's what you meant by disclosing your reasons only at the highest level?"

"Yes. I'd see the Home Secretary himself, if necessary, but he'd take the advice of the judge. Wait a bit." He relapsed once again into thought. "Yes, I think you'd better come with me, like last time we saw Sir George. You may have to do a spot or two of explaining and I'd rather you did it than I."

He looked at me sharply. "It's a pity you can't get one of the bigwigs of your profession to back you, Mark," he said seriously. "I think you're the first sane psychiatrist I've ever met. But if we had the backing of one of the gentlemen who grace public gatherings, it would do us a lot of good."

"There's Dinborough," I said, thinking rapidly. "He's been a good friend to me in various ways. He might be induced to back us."

"Sir Gilbert Dinborough, the Royal physician?" Guy asked. When I nodded, he smiled and continued: "He'd certainly be a good man if you can get him. In that case you'd better go after your man instead of coming with me. Meanwhile I'll go after the judge. In this way we'll get two birds with one stone, as the saying goes."

"Very well. That seems a sound scheme and it'll probably save time in the end."

"That's understood, then," he said, rising from his chair. "And now I'm going. I'll say only this, Mark: I'm glad I came. I've got more hope now than I ever had before."

"It's heartening to hear you say so," I returned.

In a few minutes I was alone once more and I ran over the whole affair. Of course, I knew the risk we were taking – or rather I knew what the risk would be if we were allowed to take it. It might so easily lead, as Dick's additional findings had, to still further proof against Veronica. It was certainly a risk, but I was more than willing to face it, because I had now got to the stage that I had to know the truth, whatever the consequences.

What was more important was that Guy did not accept the police's new evidence. He believed, as I did, that the whole affair was some ghastly and tragic mistake, the correction of which could not come by conventional methods.

Nothing could have done more to establish confidence in myself than Guy's support; and he was not content to leave it at that. The very next day he was going to begin another and, as I hoped, the final round of the contest by making a direct appeal to the highest authorities. So far, the fight had gone against us on points. In this last round we hoped, with something more than mere desperation, that we would restore the balance by delivering a knock-out.

My thoughts returned to my share in the forthcoming proceedings. I had to see Sir Gilbert Dinborough, a man whose judgement I trusted and who was looked upon as one of the first half-dozen consulting physicians in London. It would not be easy to gain his support, but at the same time he would not withhold it simply because it might lead him into a questionable position. If he could be brought honestly to accept my theory, he would willingly come into the open and add his immense prestige to our cause. That would be a vast help; but as I made my way to bed, feeling more restful in spirit than I had for many a long day, it was a possibility I barely dared to contemplate.

EIGHTEEN

It was soon after ten o'clock when I telephoned Sir Gilbert Dinborough's secretary. She was not at all encouraging, but when I pressed that it was a very urgent matter, she promised to refer it to Sir Gilbert himself when he arrived during the course of the next half hour or so. With that I had to be content.

It was nearly half past eleven when the telephone rang. I leapt to it hoping it might be Dinborough, but it turned out to be Guy. He said he hadn't been able to see the judge yet, but was hoping to do so next day. I told him, in turn, of how things stood at my end of the business.

"You must remember that what is important to us doesn't really matter a damn to these people. The higher up you are the more you can afford to disregard other people's affairs. But we'll win through." He added directions as to where he was to be found and than rang off, while I resumed my waiting.

An hour later I was beginning to wonder if I had better telephone Dinborough again. I knew secretaries and their promises of referring matters to their employers; my own made frequent use of the device to ward off importunate callers. Yet I hardly thought it would apply in this case. After all I was no stranger to Sir Gilbert. He had helped me a lot in my early days of specialization and he had always shown himself friendly and sympathetic, even when he was unable to offer any particular assistance. For the moment I decided not to make a second call.

It was as well that I made that decision. Just after a quarter to one Sir Gilbert himself rang.

"Sorry if I've kept you waiting, Harding," he said as soon as I answered the phone. "I just came in this morning, got your message, but I couldn't telephone you then because of an urgent consultation. What is it you want?"

"Your help, Sir Gilbert," I replied, knowing he liked direct answers.

"I see. Well come round to my club in half an hour and we'll lunch together."

"That's exceedingly kind of you, Sir Gilbert," I returned.

"Then I shall meet you at the club." He rang off abruptly. That was typical of him.

I knew his club – one of those depressing old-fashioned establishments in Pall Mall with its ornate entrance hall, its gilded pilasters and its ferns. I arrived there quarter of an hour earlier. Sir Gilbert nodded to me when he came in, led me to sign the Visitor's Book and then we proceeded straight to the dining-room and took up seats at a corner table near a window. The meal was, like the ferns, typical of the club – solid, satisfying and deadly dull.

Over the coffee he looked at me with disconcerting keenness. "Now, Harding, tell me about your troubles," he said. "I hope it isn't a serious trouble. That field of yours is rather risky, you know, but let's hear it."

"It's not professional trouble, Sir Gilbert," I replied. "It's more personal than that and I expect you already know something about it. My name's been quite prominently, of late, in the daily press."

"Veronica Lloyd – your fiancée?" He lowered his eyebrows as though trying to remember. "Isn't she accused of having supposedly killed a man?"

"Yes and ..."

"Oh, yes," he interrupted me. "Yes, I remember it now. It was your name that attracted my attention. I'm not interested in murder cases as a rule."

"I can see you know about the case, then," I observed. Without more preamble I plunged into a condensed account of the whole affair, bringing out those points which had the most direct bearing on the favour I was going to ask him.

He looked as though he was about to interrupt me, but he held himself in check and when I came to the last phase and the application we were now making on Veronica's behalf, his eyes opened wide.

"A horrible experience for you and the girl," he commented when at last I had finished. "But she seems to have good friends. And you think this experiment of yours is likely to succeed?"

"If I put it as a fifty-fifty chance, I should probably be exaggerating," I answered quietly. "But even if the odds were heavily against success, I think it should be undertaken. At any rate, we should never be able to reproach ourselves with having seen a possible way and failed to take it."

"That's true. Even a negative result in an experiment has its value. And where do I come into this?"

I told him, stressing the value of authority. Sir Gilbert listened quietly and a grim smile crossed his mouth.

"The idea is that I should sponsor this very doubtful undertaking – is that it?" he remarked and then chuckled. "What do you think my colleagues would say if I appeared in public in support of these psychological flights?"

"I don't think that would trouble you unduly, Sir Gilbert," I returned, smiling. "The only point is whether you yourself believe the experiment worth while."

His eyes twinkled. "You seem to know me, young man," he said. "But you're right. Now give me time to think it over and ask you a few questions. Let's go into the lounge."

After we'd seated ourselves on two deep leather armchairs, he thought for a while and then began to ask me about the ideas I had proposed. His questions were very searching and I had to confess my ignorance to some of them. At the end of the ordeal – and an ordeal it certainly was – Sir Gilbert relaxed again into thought.

Then he raised himself slightly in his chair.

"Before I tell you what I've decided," he said abruptly, "go along to the telephone and find out what this barrister friend of yours has been doing. I want to find out how the land lies."

I did as I was told. Luckily, Guy himself answered the telephone. He was able to report some progress. He had seen the judge, who told him he would look into the matter and would give him his answer in due course.

With this not too encouraging news, I returned to Sir Gilbert who turned towards me as I approached his chair.

"Well?" he asked.

I told him and he nodded.

"I'm not surprised. You ought to know that our judges are a very conservative lot – some of them at any rate. However, let me have a go."

"You?" I said, staggered.

"Yes," he replied. "I happen to know Judge Falkirk quite well. I am also interested in this experiment of yours from the purely scientific angle. Don't give yourself ideas. I take a special pleasure in watching other people make fools of themselves."

Still chuckling he made his way to the telephone from which I had just emerged. He spent some time in there and when he came back he was smiling.

"We are seeing my friend, the judge, at four o'clock, when no doubt in accordance with British custom, we shall be provided with a cup of tea. Ring up your barrister friend and tell him to meet us at my Harley Street rooms at a quarter to four."

I was too astonished to speak, but I managed to pull myself together, thank him and rush into the phone box again. Guy, like me, seemed overwhelmed at first, but he recovered to utter a whoop of joy.

"It's a break at last," he said. "Let's hope it'll last."

I agreed with him.

Chief Justice Sir John Falkirk was a tall, spare man, with the face and manner of a Cambridge don. He greeted Guy formally and shook hands with Dinborough very warmly and responded coldly to the latter's introduction of myself.

"I owe you an apology, Dinborough," he said in a quiet firm voice. "I didn't realise that you were interested in this affair. Mr. Hereward saw me yesterday but did not mention that you were interested personally."

Dinborough smiled quizzically. "When Hereward saw you yesterday, he had no confirmation of my interest," he said. "There were various technical questions still to be discussed with my colleague Dr. Harding, and I could not allow my name to be mentioned till I was fully satisfied. I am here now because I am fully satisfied."

It was a neat and impressive introduction to the business in hand and I thought how lucky I had been to gain this man's support. Not only was he a fine physician, but he was obviously an adept in handling men and affairs.

"I am a very busy person," said Judge Falkirk, after we had settled down, "contrary to the popular belief about judges. Shall we, Mr. Hereward, discuss again this new idea of yours?"

Guy began the discussion, pointing out that the idea was not originally his but mine. He had made a brilliant little speech, marshalling the facts with his accustomed force and lucidity that made the judge smile faintly, and I noticed a look of approval in Dinborough's eyes, though in the main he assumed that immobile mask I had seen before.

Judge Falkirk nodded when Guy finished.

"The case is more than familiar to me," he said. "I've considered the special circumstances in which the murder was supposedly perpetrated. I can only say that at the moment it'll rest with the jury and my direction to them, after hearing the whole evidence in Court."

"We understand that, Your Honour," said Guy. "Our position is that we are asking for permission to carry out a certain experiment in order to secure fresh evidence, which, if obtained, may well alter the entire nature of the case and bring about either an acquittal or a dismissal of the case altogether."

"That is the crux of the whole matter," put in Sir Gilbert. "Some very important medical points are raised by this case and they are ones which so far as I can see have important medico-legal bearings. The fact that they do not seem to have arisen before makes it all the more necessary, in my view, that the experiment should be carried out. There is the immediate object of establishing the truth and perhaps saving an innocent woman from unjust punishment. There is also the wider implication; I regard it as a test case."

Judge Falkirk remained for a moment silent.

"Why wasn't this raised earlier?" he asked. "I am in a rather difficult position. It is not for me to say what is and what is not a test case. Moreover, I am not sure that this is a test case in the legal sense. It may be to you medical gentlemen. But there again, I have to point out that it is not the function of the judiciary to provide opportunities for medical research by making available persons who are already indicted for murder."

Guy glanced at Dinborough, who nodded.

"Excuse me, Your Honour," said Guy, having taken a deep breath. "I think, if you will forgive me, you are taking a slightly distorted view of our purpose here. We are not seeking to conduct an experiment for its own sake. Our position is that we believe – and we have eminent support for our belief in the presence here of Sir Gilbert – that there are certain hitherto unknown facts in this case which can be revealed, if they exist, only by the process of a psychological experiment. That experiment demands the co-operation of the accused woman, Veronica Lloyd. We ask that we may, under conditions of strict control and proper safeguards, have access to Miss Lloyd for the conduct of that experiment, and, if it yields the results we believe it may, we then propose to bring this new evidence at the time of the trial."

"Yes, I do understand that," said Falkirk, relaxing a little. "But I had to define my own position and not run the risk of being accused of partiality – that no judge can afford. You do see this point of mine!"

"I think, Falkirk," said Dinborough quietly, "you can put away from you any suspicion of that kind. These two gentlemen have devoted exceptional care and a vast amount of work to this case to ensure that justice is served. I, myself, am convinced that the method Dr. Harding proposes is a sound one. The case is unusual and unusual procedures are necessary if it is to be cleared up. I think you will agree with me when I say that while we all recognize the validity of the judge's impartiality, it is nevertheless part of his duties to see that no gross miscarriage of justice takes place."

"Yes. A judge can act if there is such a possibility, but only when such action does not obstruct the normal process of investigation."

"Yes, Your Honour," said Guy. "That is, of course, understood. That brings us back to the point I made just now that our application is solely for assisting the functioning of the normal legal procedure."

"Very well," said Judge Falkirk. "Let us see what Dr. Harding has to offer." He turned towards me. "Will you proceed, Dr. Harding, please?"

As simply as I could I told Judge Falkirk the whole of my theory and what had led up to it. He listened with the closest attention and he gave me the impression that beneath the judge's formal mask there lay a very keen and intelligent personality – as indeed, might have been expected, for Chief Justices are men of quite exceptional ability and integrity.

"I confess I find myself in an awkward position," he said after a pause. "If the facts are as you state them, then I would feel obliged to grant your application. At the same time – if you will forgive me, Dr. Harding – your theory or proposal, whatever you like to call it, sounds a trifle far-fetched to me. Therefore, to have to decide between my own doubts, which, I think, are those that any layman would feel, and the authority of Sir Gilbert and yourself, Dr. Harding, I think I should consult our own medical advisers."

"Yes, Your Honour," said Guy quickly. "I quite agree with you, but may I remind you that the matter is of the utmost urgency if we're to spare an innocent woman further suffering."

"That is a weighty point," the judge replied. And then he smiled broadly. "You are asking a great deal of me in all ways, gentlemen. Surely you should remember that this court is one which looks unfavourably on speed?"

His smile and our answering ones – Dinborough chuckled – lightened the whole atmosphere.

"I think I see what we can do," he said. "It may be that a human life – an innocent human life – is at stake, but I do feel that we must have adequate safeguards against creating a dangerous precedent. What I suggest, then, is that I make arrangements for you to see Sir James Shelsdon, our pathologist, at once. If he agrees that you have made out a responsible case then you shall have the application for which you ask."

My heart leapt for joy. This sudden decision was as unexpected as it was welcome.

"Thank you, Your Honour," said Guy sincerely, "I don't know how to express my gratitude for your consideration."

"There are one or two other points that occurred to me," went on the judge. "If a release is made there have to be proper safeguards, as you yourself, Mr. Hereward, have suggested. The experiment, if it takes place, shall be made in the presence of two police officers – one the inspector in charge of the case, the other some high ranking officer nominated by the Commissioner. Do you agree, Dr. Harding? You think it feasible?"

"The presence of too many people might be a complicating factor," I replied, "but the condition is quite reasonable. Might I suggest, as witnesses must be present, that there should also be two competent medical witnesses among them and add that they might be Sir Gilbert here, if he agrees, and Sir James Shelsdon?"

"That is a sound suggestion," admitted Judge Falkirk. "Do you accept, Dinborough?"

"Yes, it's quite acceptable to me," replied Sir Gilbert. "I should hate to be left out, having gone so far."

"That detail can be taken as settled." The judge suddenly smiled. "The other point is an example of official caution. If the experiment takes place, I shall arrange for the release to be for medical examination by the accused woman's own doctors. I do not wish the whole truth of this business to be spread too soon."

"That's a good idea," said Dinborough.

"Very well, then," Judge Falkirk said. "I shall ring Shelsdon now and see if you can go straight to him. If he gives his approval, I shall at once issue the necessary instructions and the accused shall be brought to any address you name within the London area. Where would it be?" he asked, turning to me.

"My consulting rooms," I replied, giving him my card. "The accused is familiar with them and will feel at ease there. That is something which may help the work considerably. Besides it will give colour to the suggestion of medical examination."

This time Judge Falkirk chuckled. He did not say anything more but lifted his telephone. In a few seconds he was through to Sir James Shelsdon and ten minutes later we were on our way to see the great Home Office pathologist.

NINETEEN

I looked at my watch. It was exactly half past eight. In another half hour, I thought, I shall see Veronica. Deep in my heart I dismissed the idea of failure. My confidence in my theory was unshaken. I had won Dinborough's approval and finally, after a long and exhausting discussion, Sir James Shelsdon had been won to our side. When I explained my theory to him he was definitely against it. But in the end, after a magnificent appeal by Dinborough, he had relented. Dinborough's invocation of his scientific curiosity won the day.

I was looking out of the window when the receptionist was ushering in the first two visitors. One was Dick Morris, still looking very tired and worn out. The other, to my great surprise, was the Commissioner himself.

"I did not expect to see you here, Sir George," I remarked when I had greeted him.

"My instructions were that I should nominate a high ranking officer to accompany Inspector Morris," he replied, "so I nominated myself. Besides, I'm very interested about this – er – medical examination." His eyes twinkled.

"There is no one else I would rather see here," I said. "Can we wait for the arrival of the others before I outline the procedure we propose to adopt?"

"Certainly," said Sir George. "We are in your hands."

I looked at my watch. It was eight-thirty precisely. At ten

minutes to nine all the rest of the party arrived. This consisted of Dinborough and Guy, followed by Sir James Shelsdon who was only a minute late.

After the usual greetings, I began to talk.

"Now, gentlemen," I said, "I'm going to tell you what we propose to do in the way of a general plan. If you have any objections, we will modify the arrangements as you think fit." I paused for a moment then went on. "I have given instructions that Miss Lloyd shall be shown into an ante-room with her attendants. She does not know what is afoot and it is essential that she should not be subjected to any sudden surprises, which might put her in a frame of mind that would militate against our success. For this reason I shall ask Sir George to allow me a preliminary interview with the accused, in the presence of one witness, naturally. Inspector Morris, who knows the accused well, would be the ideal witness for the purpose."

Sir George nodded quickly. "I agree to that course," he said and instructed Dick Morris to that effect.

"The actual experiment will take place in this room," I went on. "Before I bring in Miss Lloyd I want you to withdraw to those chairs at the far end and be the passive observers. Of course, you can take any notes you wish of all that passes. That is all." I looked round at the little circle.

"Any questions, gentlemen?"

"None," said Sir George and the others nodded.

"Good. Now I propose to tell you in more detail what I intend to do."

There was silence in the room but I could see that all of them were interested to hear about what was going to happen.

"You know that Hereward and I are not at all convinced that the facts of this case were correctly interpreted. The contention has been that Miss Lloyd killed Samuel Laing while she was in a somnambulistic trance. We hold that she did not commit the murder thus or indeed at all, but that she was present at the time in a state of trance. The object of this experiment is to try to bring to the surface, by hypnotic suggestion, the latest memories of the experience that must be in her unconscious. I believe that it will be possible to do so. And if we can bring out anything, it will be the naked truth. To avoid any suggestion of trickery of any kind, I am going to ask Sir James and Sir Gilbert, when the time comes, to examine Miss Lloyd and satisfy themselves that she is in a state of hypnotic trance."

"Just one point, Harding," said Sir George. "Suppose Miss Lloyd confesses to the crime – what then?"

"The fact will be established beyond any shadow of a doubt." My tone was grim. "We are taking a grave risk from our own point of view in making this experiment, but I think you will agree that either way it will be justified. At the same time," I warned, "it may be that we shall get no results at all. I do not know about Miss Lloyd's hypnotic suggestibility and she might prove to be one of those people who cannot be induced into the hypnotic state."

"One other point," continued Sir George. "You mentioned the word 'suggestibility'. Does that mean that you can suggest to her what you want her to say?"

"No. I can suggest to her that she can take a certain course of action, which must be in accord with her innate wishes. In this case it will be to tell the story of the crime. I cannot put words in her mouth. I ask my two eminent colleagues here to vouch to you for my sincerity and also to confirm my statements."

Both Sir Gilbert and Sir James expressed their agreement and I waited for the next question. But none came. In the silence that pervaded the room I heard a car stop outside. After what seemed an age, the receptionist came in.

"The lady and two other women have arrived, sir," she announced. Veronica and her escort! I rose and left the room. Inspector Morris followed at my sign.

As I walked towards the room in which Veronica was waiting, my mind was a sudden vortex. The whole thing was so unreal, a terrible nightmare after all. Yes, I thought, Veronica was waiting for me and later we were going out to lunch together in the old familiar way ... Then Dick's form broke through to my consciousness and I recognized that I was indeed day-dreaming and the ugly truth was reality.

That short corridor was like an endless tunnel to me and when I finally reached the end of it, it needed a mental effort for me to turn the handle. I steadied myself and pushed the door gently.

There was Veronica. She was wearing the same suit she had worn on the night of her arrest. Her face was pale and composed, though she seemed a little puzzled at finding herself in my consulting rooms. By her side were two women, obviously plain-clothes police officers, who came to attention as Dick and I walked in.

"You had better leave us," said Dick to them. "Where shall they go, Mark?"

"The room next door," I replied, not moving my eyes from Veronica.

She had had her head cast downwards as we entered. She had not looked up. But now as she heard my voice, she slowly raised it and our eyes met. A little colour crept into those pale, worn cheeks. Her lips parted slightly and her breathing deepened a little and her hands clenched.

Veronica! I thought. This is my Veronica. I feasted on her with my eyes. A wild impulse to seize her and make away came over me, but I fought it down. I had to keep calm, or I might be unable to do the one thing that held in it a chance of restoring to her her freedom and her happiness. Never before had she needed me so much as now! For her sake, I must control these urges which possessed me.

That moment will remain for ever in me as the most memorable in my career. There was sweetness in it too: the sweetness of seeing again the woman I loved. There was poignancy in it, for here she was and I was helpless to take her away. Above all there was a heavy sense of responsibility that induced in me a curious and yet stimulating humility. For now in the last extremity she relied on me and on me alone. She did not know it. I alone knew it and that made my responsibility towards her all the greater.

In the corridor I had been besieged by doubts. I had even regretted suggesting this experiment which might so easily fail and make a great tragedy darker still. I doubted my own powers to do what I had set out to do. But now all those doubts fell away from me. I had to do it – for Veronica's sake. A new confidence welled up in me. I should do it even if it were to be my last professional act!

Slowly I disengaged my eyes from hers.

"Veronica," I said.

"Mark," she replied.

That was all. Again our eyes met. In hers was a puzzled question that I could read at once. What was she doing here? What fresh trick of fate was being played on her? And how came I to be mixed up with it?

I think she feared that she was to be examined with a view to her being certified as insane and that may have accounted for the fear I saw in her face. I tried to make my own face expression soothing and reassuring. I was glad to see that I had succeeded, for her bearing lightened a little and there was even the shadow of a smile on her lips.

"You want to know why you are here," I said, forcing myself to be calm and professional-like. "I cannot tell you everything, darling, but only that we have had a great fight to get you here at all. No, you are not going to be certified – I feel that is what you dread. I ask you to place yourself entirely in my hands. Don't question anything I do. Trust me, Veronica, trust me for old time's sake!"

"I trust you, Mark," she replied in a low voice. "How wonderful to hear you say 'darling' again."

I resisted the impulse to seize her in my arms. "Listen, dear. In a moment I am going to take you into my consulting room. There are several people there, including Guy, but I want you to try and forget all about them. I am going to ask you to sit upon the couch and let me hypnotize you. Don't ask me why. I can't tell you now. Only believe that it is vitally important to you and to me. That is all. Do your best to co-operate. Don't struggle against it. Let yourself go. And then, when you are yourself again, you may well find that your feet are firmly planted on the road to freedom."

"Yes, darling," she replied. "I'll do my best although I don't understand anything. I just know that I must trust you."

"And now," I smiled, "I'm going to do something that has nothing to do with this business and is probably irregular and unethical. But our friend Dick will forget it."

I took her into my arms and kissed her – a long, lingering kiss that had in it something of dedication as though it sealed a pledge made between us. And as at last I disengaged myself from her embracing arms, I knew that, if I failed and Veronica must go to prison probably for life, my life, too, would come to an end. For her freedom was my freedom and my life without her was not worth living.

"Come, Veronica, let's get it over," I said, trying to be as casual as possible. Taking her hand, I led her along the passage into my consulting-room. It was a walk to paradise – or to hell.

TWENTY

When Veronica entered the room, she took one glance at the little cluster of men at the far end of the room, smiled slightly at Guy and then remained silent. Dick tiptoed to the chair near the one on which the Commissioner was sitting. Then I asked her to sit on the couch and the experiment was going to begin. I felt remarkably calm and self-possessed now. Nothing mattered any more except the task in hand.

When I saw that she was comfortably settled, I crossed to the window and drew the heavy curtains. A shade lamp burnt on my desk, giving a soft mellow light. Then I switched on a bright light at the foot of the couch.

"Look at this light!" I commanded. "Concentrate on it. It won't hurt your eyes."

She obeyed, wincing a little at first at its brightness, but she held her gaze steadily. While she stared at the light I spoke to her softly. I have found this the best of all ways of hypnotism. In psychological work, the psychologist should withdraw his own personality as much as possible, for no one knows to the full the manifold ways in which the power of one mind may communicate itself to another. There is ample evidence of some form of communication between hypnotist and hypnotized which we call telepathy. And now I wanted no suggestion that I had imposed my own thoughts on hers. I knew that I was being watched by two medical men who would not hesitate to denounce me if they suspected the faintest trace of trickery.

For a little while I was worried. Failure so soon? Veronica kept moving a little as though her conscious will refused to yield to the suggestions I was making. But then she grew quiescent and after a few moments more I noticed that she was gazing fixedly at the bright light, without discomfort and with pupils widely dilated.

I drew a deep breath. The crucial phase was passed. The hypnotic state had been induced.

I signed to Sir Gilbert and Sir James who were ready for it. They came forward quietly and bent over Veronica, applying all the usual tests and satisfying themselves that the trance was genuine. They took their time and I was glad that they omitted nothing. Finally, they nodded and retired to the end of the room without speaking a word.

When I spoke again, my voice seemed to echo round the room. I had the impression as if the whole world was listening.

"Do you remember that last night you went to see Samuel Laing by going along the balcony?"

She did not answer and I repeated the question.

"Yes," she answered quietly. "I remember it. It was horrible." Her voice had that curious characterless monotone which marks all speech in hypnotism.

"Can you recall what happened?"

"Yes," came the answer. Her voice was clearer now and I knew that the listeners could hear it. It was very satisfactory.

"Then tell me what happened," I prompted.

She paused and then began to speak.

"I was in bed ... I thought of Samuel and there was Mark, too. Samuel stood between Mark and me and I had to get him out of the way. Somehow he had to go ... There was that knife I bought ... I could kill him ..."

Her voice trailed away into silence. I was aware of a cold sweat on my brow. It looked like a confession after all! As she remained silent I gently suggested to her that she should continue. After a further brief pause, she resumed.

"It was a terrible idea, but he wanted to hurt Mark, to smash his career ... I must kill him ... I must."

A tremor passed through her body and for a moment I thought that the hypnosis was passing. But after a short silence she took up the tale again. There was a subtle change and I knew then that we should hear the truth. Veronica was speaking now in the present tense. In her unconscious she was re-living, as I had hoped she would, the whole of that tragic night. Yet even as success seemed assured, I trembled, for I did not know yet what the scene would be.

"I must kill him ... The knife is in the drawer. Yes, that's the one ... He's sleeping now ... This is the time I always used to go to him, the monster ..."

Then, to my surprise, she rose slowly from the couch. My heart missed a beat. She was re-enacting the whole thing, even to the point of walking. Never before had I seen a hypnotized subject take to motor action. It was a profound shock.

She moved surely to a little distance from the couch and stooped down, making movements as though she was taking something from the drawer. I could feel the intent stares of eyes from the end of the room, as the observers concentrated their whole attention.

Now she had come to my desk and picked up a ruler that lay on it. She carried it delicately. And she held it as though it were a dagger point upwards. Silently she moved along, lifting her feet as though to pass over a step, as she must have done to pass out through the window. After a few more steps, she again raised her feet. Now she was in Laing's room. The whole thing was uncanny, frightening, even to me who had so often used a hypnotic technique.

Suddenly she screamed. The sound echoed round the room with a terrifying intensity. One could feel with her the horror of what she saw. For she obviously saw something. Her eyes were fixed and staring.

"He's dead ... dead ... someone has killed him ... Oh God!" She screamed again.

I could almost have screamed with her. What the emotions of the observers were I don't know, though Guy told me – and he is not a nervy man – that he felt he wanted to shield his eyes so that he could not see what was happening. Naked fear was in the room.

"He's gone ... Samuel's dead ... That knife in his chest ..." Veronica returned to the couch, bending over as though someone was lying there. Then she let the ruler drop to the floor. Its impact with the ground sounded like an explosion in the tense silence.

Now she reached across and began tugging at something. So that was it! She was removing the knife from Laing's chest. Though she held nothing in her hand, her grasp was unmistakable. She was gripping the haft of a knife. For a moment or two she stood looking down, holding the invisible weapon in her hand a little distance from the couch.

"No, he's dead ... Did I kill him? ..." She looked downwards and saw the ruler. "No, that's my knife ... I must get rid of this or they will think I did it ... Did I? No! No, no! ..."

Veronica's stride was quicker now. She stumbled rather than stepped over the ledge onto the imaginary balcony and then hurled that non-existing knife away from her. More slowly she paced back and dropped onto the couch.

"Dead – dead – dead," she moaned. "Dead in his sleep. He's dead ... Oh God, what shall I do? ..." She began to sob a little and then lay quiet for a space. Suddenly she raised her head. "The bell ... the doorbell ... It's Samuel ... No he's dead ..."

I detected signs of danger. This relived experience was too intense for her. That sometimes happens in hypnosis, which is a dangerous, double-edged weapon.

I had no wish for her to go through the pain of that first interview with Inspector Morris when he called – and it was to that her unconscious was moving.

"That is enough," I said quietly but firmly. "You can forget what followed. You must rest now. There is nothing to fear. Everything will be all right when you awake."

"Yes," she said.

Her tense body relaxed a little and very carefully I resettled her on the couch. Then I silently moved to the door and opened it. I beckoned to the others to follow me. We all went into the next room. Then I sent the receptionist to look after Veronica.

"She will probably be a little weak and shocked when she wakes," I said. "Have a hot drink ready and try to make her comfortable. You know what to do."

The girl nodded and I went to rejoin the others.

It was a good five minutes before any of us spoke. I scrutinized the serious faces about me.

Then again I felt silent and terribly exhausted. It was Sir James Shelsdon who spoke first. He came towards me and grasped my hand.

"Congratulations, Harding," he said with deep sincerity. "It has been a most remarkable experience. As you know, I've always been sceptical of hypnosis, but now – well, I shall have to alter my mind."

"Yes," commented Dinborough, "it was an experience indeed that needed some courage to carry out. It must have been utterly exhausting for you. The main thing is, though, that you have at last proved your point. I think Miss Lloyd's innocence has now been clearly established."

"May I return to a point I raised earlier?" asked Sir George. "I mean, can we accept this remarkable performance as genuine?"

"Most definitely yes," said Sir James Shelsdon.

"I'm seconding that," Dinborough remarked. "All the way."

"Well, I'm prepared to be guided by you, gentlemen," acknowledged the Commissioner, "but being convinced myself doesn't mean that the Court will accept it too. We still have to face the other circumstances."

"It will be difficult, Sir George," Guy said, turning towards the Commissioner. "I think the next move lies with your department."

"How is that?"

"You are, as we all here are, convinced of the innocence of Miss Lloyd. So is Inspector Morris, who once said that the case was one of murder with an eye-witness who couldn't speak. His eye-witness has spoken. The murder was done not by Miss Lloyd, but by some person or persons unknown. The police must have another attempt to establish the identity of that person."

"I agree with you, Hereward, wholeheartedly," Sir George smiled. "Inspector Morris'll have to try once again – third time lucky, perhaps. It has to be."

Dick who was listening said eagerly, "Yes, Sir George, it'll be damn difficult, but I'll try and hope that this, my third attempt, will indeed by lucky."

"Yes," Sir George nodded. "It has to be, Morris!" He looked round. "Anything else?"

We looked at each other and we all shook our heads. For myself I felt too weak for discussion and so, I believe, did the others. I suggested that the party adjourned and this seemed to meet with general approval.

"One thing before we go," said Sir James suddenly. "We have to decide what to do with Miss Lloyd. She is still under suspicion of murder and cannot be granted bail. But this was a visit for medical examination and we, the medicos, agree that she is suffering from extreme nervous exhaustion."

"That's quite true," answered Sir Gilbert.

"In that case, gentlemen, I'll see to it that an order is made that Miss Lloyd be sent to the prison hospital for special care – very special care," he added with a slight smile. "Meanwhile, perhaps Dr. Harding will grant my department the hospitality of his rooms and allow Miss Lloyd to remain here, under guard, of course, to comply with the formalities, till a separate ward in the hospital can be prepared for her."

"Certainly, Sir James, I do," I said. Though I knew I must not see her, it was joy to me to know Veronica could remain under my roof for a little longer. And my heart warmed to Sir James Shelsdon, the man who, according to the popular Press, dealt only with those things that brought life imprisonment to the murderer. Now he was bringing new life to the innocent. I went up to him and, in grateful silence, wrung his hand. He smiled at me. He is one more friend this ghastly affair has brought to Veronica and me.

TWENTY-ONE

I kept myself as much as I could in the background, following the experiment with Veronica. My part in the case was over. Nevertheless, it brought some unexpected problems. Sir Gilbert Dinborough, who was on the council of the Royel College of Physicians, invited me to read a paper before the Society of Medicine, and dropped a hint that it might easily lead to my being elected a Fellow of the College. In other circumstances I would have been proud to accept it, but I declined. This had been no brilliant piece of psychiatry to me; it had been forced on me by events every one of which I hated. I did not want to make the ordeal Veronica had undergone a means of advancement in my career.

I was allowed to see Veronica in the hospital. For some time she was dazed and not in full control of herself. Under skilled care, however, she recovered slowly and it was a heart-warming sight to watch the old colour creeping gradually back into her cheeks.

When she was well enough, Dick and I saw her together and told her the truth. The story seemed to surprise her. She remained silent for a moment and then shook her head. Even today she cannot quite understand what happened.

At this time, too, I saw little of Guy. He was wrapped up in legal problems and worried not a little about the trial. We had left only about two weeks before the day of the trial and as it seemed Dick was not making very much headway in the investigations. He certainly had not collected sufficient factual evidence to place in the hands of the defence.

Guy called on me and asked me if I would give evidence if necessary.

"I want to keep the whole of the experiment out of the Court if I can," he said. "I'm still not satisfied that it would convince the Court of Veronica's innocence. And besides, it would provide the Press with a first-class sensation that would be painful to us all – and particularly to Veronica. But if the worst comes to the worst, I shall have to put you on the witness stand."

"Very well," I replied without enthusiasm. "But let's hope that Dick will have a stroke of luck soon."

"I don't envy him his job, but when last I saw him – that was yesterday – he seemed a bit more hopeful. I'm not really interested now whether he gets the actual murderer. My only concern is to get Veronica free at the earliest possible moment. We have to convince the judge of her innocence – that's all that matters now."

"The sooner you get Veronica out, the better I shall be pleased," I replied with vigour.

"As I said before, we've to convince the judge," Guy replied. "That's why you have to go on the stand, Mark. It'll be rather nasty publicity, but we've to face it if all else fails."

So the matter ended for the time being.

A few days later Inspector Morris called on me and gave me a brief account of his new line of investigation. The chief item was that the second knife found outside the Laing's balcony was now identified as the fatal weapon. Dick had insisted that the experts re-examine it.

"Yes, Mark," he smiled at me. "For the first time in this dreadful affair our luck held. In spite of the fact that the most prominent fingerprints were those of Veronica, the experts were able to identify that they were superimposed on a number of others."

"Were those lower ones also Veronica's?" I asked in anxiety.

"No, definitely not," Dick replied. "After elaborate tests, they all came not only to the conclusion that they were not Veronica's, but also they produced fingerprints that the police had no difficulty in identifying as those of a man known to us – an old friend whose fingerprints have been recorded in the Central Record Office for quite a long time." Dick laughed heartily this time.

"Thank God for that!" I almost shouted. "Did you get the man?"

"Oh, yes," said Dick. "As a matter of fact, we'd had him already in custody for some time on a series of other charges. And do you know what?"

"Go on, Dick!" I prompted. "Is he connected with the murder of Samuel Laing?"

"And how," Dick answered. "At first he denied having had any connection with Laing. But then we were able to identify several anonymous letters threatening Laing and blackmailing him as being written by our man. When confronted with them, he had to admit that he was the author of the letters."

"But what about the murder?" I asked.

"I think he's our man, Mark," Dick said. "We know that he'd dealings with Laing of a very dubious nature and they have often quarrelled violently with our man getting always the wrong end of the stick."

As Inspector Morris went on with his narrative I realised that a new picture of the crime had come to light and for which ample and incontrovertible evidence was available. It was proved that this man was in Laing's room at the night of the murder. The fatal dagger also was identified as belonging to him. It appeared that while he was actually mortally stabbing Samuel Laing, Veronica entered the room by way of the balcony in a state of somnambulistic trance and carrying the dagger. At the sight of the man bending over the deceased and of the knife projecting from his chest, she screamed and dropped the dagger she held in her hand. The man escaped and Veronica then, still in a state of trance, withdrew the knife from the body of Samuel Laing thinking, in her abnormal state, that she might save his life. Or perhaps fearing that she might have killed him, she disposed of the knife by throwing it over the balcony rail. Thus her fingerprints were superimposed on those of the actual murderer.

All this account of the actual murder sounded at first incredible to me, but Dick Morris assured me that he already had the confession of the man.

"Did he actually confess, Dick?" I asked.

"Yes," he answered. "Of course, at the beginning he tried to pretend that it was quite the opposite. He came to see Laing because of some urgent deal and surprised Veronica with the dagger in her hand bending over Samuel Laing."

"Then how did you make him admit that he did the killing?" I pressed Dick.

"Oh, we've our methods, Mark," he smiled but did not elaborate on his assertion. I did not press him further. The main thing was that Veronica, my Veronica, would be free.

By an order of the Attorney-General, also called, evidence against Veronica was dismissed and she was let free immediately.

Of course, the usual suggestion of a financial recompense was made, but Veronica turned it down unhesitatingly. Not all the money in the world could compensate for her agony and the long and terrible torture of an innocent woman.

I myself stopped my friend Dick Morris from apologizing on behalf of the police for the blunder they had committed. I told him that nobody in the world could blame them – certainly not I or Veronica. Who could say the police acted unfairly? The case against Veronica was clear-cut and unanswerable because of the evidence at hand. Her case should become a classic as an example of the morass into which the trail of circumstantial evidence can lead.

It was ten o'clock in the morning when I drove my Jaguar to the gates of Holloway Prison. As I alighted from the car the cool autumn air brushed against my flushed face and instantly helped me to regain my self-control. It's hard to say what I did really feel. I knew, as an experienced psychiatrist, that I, of all people, should have been able to sail through what was to follow. But things don't work that way. We have a store of advice for others but who has ever found a remedy to stop the heart from beating remorselessly against one's breast in turmoil and anticipation? Even tranquillisers were scarcely adequate to calm me and, to be quite frank, I had swallowed a couple that morning. Nonetheless, here I was, excited and terribly afraid.

How would Veronica react to this first meeting with me as a free woman? How would she take it when she saw me waiting for her?

I almost ran towards her as I saw her coming out of the prison gates. I saw her before she saw me and then, waving and smiling, she cried out and ran into my outstretched arms. As I kissed her repeatedly on the mouth, the tears ran unashamedly down her cheeks. She was sobbing quietly, still smiling, and my tears too mixed with hers. All our pain and suffering seemed to melt as we held each other tightly.

"God, I must be hurting you," I laughed. "But I love you so much!" I hugged her again, not caring who was staring at us. This was the moment I had been longing for all these abysmal weeks and nothing and nobody was going to spoil it!

I took her small bundle from her hand and led her towards the car. As I placed her luggage on the rear seat, she must have seen my own suitcase.

"Are you going somewhere?" she asked in a weak, frightened voice.

"Yes, darling. WE ARE going somewhere – a place you'll love."

"I'll love any place with you, Mark." Her lips parted into a huge smile.

"But this one is special." I kissed her again and closed the car door behind her. I started the car and drove towards Esher.

Veronica seemed to recognize the landscape.

"Are we going to ... our friend's house ... the house where we first met?"

"Of course, darling. Can you suggest any better place?"

I had asked our friends to lend us their country house for the week-end. Being an inveterate sentimentalist I thought that the place where we first met and the memory of our happy life together would help her to forget all about her ordeal.

"Are we alone?" she asked as we entered the long, attractive hall and I switched on the light.

"Yes. Do you mind?"

"Darling!" she said quietly and began to cry again. "I never thought that I'd see you again ... here like this."

"From now on you must stop thinking too much – and start living!" I said softly as I ushered her into the room we both loved so much.

After relaxing for an hour or so, Veronica and I made some sandwiches and we both enjoyed the solitude of that wonderful autumn afternoon. There was so much to talk about, but on this, our first day, we chose to be silent. We just sat on the deckchairs outside in the garden patio and held hands.

That night, after dinner at a nearby restaurant, Veronica undressed and having taken a quick shower, came into the room in her thin, transparent nightgown.

I came close to her and could smell the fragrance of her body, of her hair, of her whole sensuous being. In spite of her ordeal she still looked fresh and soft and very desirable. I pressed her to me and without a word began to kiss her all over. She opened her mouth and her lips – tender and warm – and pressed them in response against my own body. I felt her arms go round my chest. I unbuttoned my pyjamas and let them drop on the floor. My body pressed on hers and we drank the pleasure of our love for a long, long time. I knew it would be like this and I was hoping that it would last for ever.

Later that night Veronica got out of bed and switched on the light. "Let's have a drink, darling. I feel very thirsty."

"Me too," I smiled, rubbing sleepy eyes. "Shall I fix us something?"

"Wine, darling. I feel I would like a nice, dry wine. Is there any?"

"Of course," I laughed. "Our hosts are very generous." I crossed to the bar in the far end of the lounge and came back holding two large glasses of champagne.

I held one out to her. "Here, darling. Let's drink to our newly-found happiness." Champagne with Veronica! I thought I had never tasted champagne like this in the whole of my life.

She emptied her glass almost in one gulp.

"Champagne!" she giggled ... "Darling, you're the most wonderful man! But ... but aren't you going to ask me?"

"To ask you what?"

"To marry you ..." her laughter echoed through the stillness of the night.

I put my empty glass down on the table. Reaching for her face I held it in both my hands cupped like a rose.

"Would you marry me, Veronica? I hope you'll say yes, because I can't imagine life without you."

The tears glistened in her eyes like minature pearls.

"Yes, Mark darling. I will marry you ... and I will love you for ever and ever." She put her arms about my neck.

I smiled and kissed her again gently this time on her soft, full lips. We drank more champagne and went back to bed. "Darling Veronica!" I whispered as I began to embrace her once more.

The following morning I telephoned my friends. They had to be the first to know.

Veronica herself prepared the dinner.

They all came. Guy, Dick and – rather surprisingly – both Sir James Shelsdon and Gilbert Dinborough. It was quite a gala occasion in its way. Of course, towards its end, when we had nearly finished the ample supply of cognac that our hosts had thoughtfully provided, talk turned to the case.

"No doubt you were right from the legal standpoint," observed Sir Gilbert, turning to Guy, "but I still feel that some tribute should have been paid in open Court to the work of our friend Mark here. It was a brilliant piece of work, that reconstruction under hypnotic trance."

"I want to forget it," I said firmly. "It's a ghastly nightmare to me. And it wasn't even original."

"How do you make that out?" asked Sir James.

"Simply because the seed of it was planted by a very talkative hypochondriac patient of mine. He set me reading 'The Moonstone' – and the plot of 'The Moonstone' isn't so very dissimilar from what happened here."

"Perhaps not," retorted Sir James. "But one can write

about things more easily than one can put them into practice."

"I certainly don't want to be the subject of a textbook on hypnosis," Veronica interposed. "I've had enough publicity to last me a lifetime. I felt like going to a plastic surgeon and having my face completely altered so that I couldn't be recognized."

"I'm glad you didn't," I said warmly.

Veronica laughed – it was good to hear her laughter.

"And yet," she continued, "there are people who go out of their way to get publicity. How they must envy me!" she said a trifle bitterly.

"Yes, the ways of the human mind are very fantastic," observed Sir Gilbert. "But you'll learn all about that soon enough when you're the wife of a psychiatrist. And that reminds me," he said, raising the huge balloon in which lay the last drops of his cognac, "shall we drink to the health of these two charming people?"

They all raised their glasses.

"To Mark and Veronica!" Sir Gilbert smiled, turning towards us.

"To Veronica and Mark!" the others of our friends responded, draining their glasses.

A week later we were married.

EPILOGUE

If I had been writing a detective story instead of trying to record a plain narrative of a searing experience, I should in an earlier chapter have introduced a character called Roderick Kyne. I should have made him sinister and cunning, turning up suddenly in odd places and getting in the way of the police, yet professing unassailable innocence.

Unfortunately, Roderick Kyne is not a bit like that. He looks what he is: a very low-grade criminal with an almost lifelong record of convictions against him, a man who has served at sea and collected the least desirable experience from the lurid quarters of the worst ports in the world. For it was Roderick Kyne who killed Samuel Laing and in the bargain nearly got a richly undeserved windfall by having poor Veronica convicted in his stead.

It was impossible to introduce him earlier into the story because no one knew of his existence as a character in the plot till the main part of it was unfolded. Inspector Morris perhaps knew of him as a regular on the Habitual Criminal Register. But it was not until after my desperate experiment with Veronica and the subsequent expert examination of the second knife that he was connected with the case.

In order not to leave any loopholes in the story of Veronica's ordeal, I think Kyne's part in it must be sketched briefly. Samuel Laing was interested in clubs of a different kind from those of the West End, where he was acknowledged proprietor. Many of the shady dens in Dockland owed their genesis to his fertile mind. And many of them were run at considerable danger to himself by this same Roderick Kyne. But whereas Kyne was a man who could not run straight and to whom crime was second nature, Samuel Laing, on the other hand, was interested solely in earning easy money. The result was that Kyne took the brunt of the business and Laing drew the profits. And Laing being what he was, he had little scruples in defrauding his brainless partner out of as much of his little share as possible.

It took a long time for Kyne's dull wits to comprehend how he was being exploited, but when he did, his reaction was in pace with his nature. Samuel Laing must die, he vowed, and death to Kyne meant the knife, of which he was a skilled user. Kyne's exploits during his sailing days had given him also a good knowledge of the tender spots in the human anatomy.

It was Kyne who killed Samuel Laing, but was quick to take advantage of Veronica's sudden appearance at the scene of the crime. He, no doubt, was hoping that the blame for the murder would be pinned on her. Yet when the pinch came and he found himself caught, he acted like the rat he was. He confessed everything – a disgusting affair of tears and abasement – to Dick Morris who was, of course, in charge of the investigations.

"This is the pattern of behaviour of all those petty criminals," Dick said to me. "They're ruthless when the going is good, but in actual fact are the basest of cowards when cornered without a chance of escaping."

There let me leave Roderick Kyne. He does not really concern my story, which is the record of Veronica's ordeal. And as far as I am concerned, I see myself as a fool who was roused to action only when it was nearly too late. I played no noble part in the affair, as Sir Gilbert tried to make out. I can never forgive myself for my blindness and weakness in the earlier stages. My only credit is that I saw the light of truth in time – but only just.

And there is a brighter side of this dark affair that I can remember with gratitude. Tragic though it was, it has brought me rewards beyond all dreams. It gave me friends – the real friends who stand by a man and who he holds dear, when all the world is arrayed against him. It gave me faith in the eternity of truth. It gave me renewed belief that even psychiatry has its practical uses in helping suffering mankind. Above all, it has given me a Veronica richer in experience, more deeply understanding of life than she could ever have been without this terrible trial – though there is nothing I would have more gladly spared her.

She is no longer Veronica Lloyd. She is Mrs. Mark Harding. It is to me at times an almost unbelievable thought. Lying on the desk in front of me is a letter addressed to 'Mrs. Mark Harding' awaiting her return from a visit to the shops. I keep glancing at it. For it is a reminder of how truly rich and fortunate I am – and also of how nearly Mrs. Mark Harding never existed.

The front door opened and Veronica came in carrying the exploits of her shopping.

"Hello," she said, depositing her parcels on the table. I walked to the bar and filled two glasses with cold, white wine.

"Here," I said, giving her a glass.

"What's the occasion?" she asked smiling.

"No special occasion. I'd just like to have a glass of wine with you, Veronica. A man as lucky as I should celebrate every day of his life." I looked at her with what could only have been absolute love.

"Darling Veronica," I smiled. She came quickly up to me, glass in her hand. I took the glass from her and put it on the little table.

"Darling Veronica," I said once more.